AFRIKA'S STRUGGLE

AFRIKA'S STRUGGLE

His Experiential Journey

KARL A. MITCHELL

ISBN: 1511621079
ISBN 13: 9781511621076
Library of Congress Control Number: 2015905506
CreateSpace Independent Publishing Platform
North Charleston, South Carolina

For my grandparents, Aston George Mitchell and Marie Louise Mitchell

ACKNOWLEDGMENTS

I AM INDEBTED to many people who gave me great feedback on *Afrika's Struggle*. However, it is not feasible to list everyone without utilizing many pages. That said, the following are of major importance:

Priscilla Schwartz, my Honors English teacher at the illustrious East Side High School, who nurtured a fifteen-year-old student's literary creativity. Under her guidance, chapter one evolved from a short story first composed for one of her assignments.

Later, at the City University of New York–Queens College, Professor Rodney Benson, Dr. Wladyslaw Rozniak, and Dr. James Jordan afforded me the opportunity to add nine more chapters to the original chapter to form the current novel via their respective mentorship.

Ms. Schwartz planted the seed, and Prof. Benson and Drs. Rozniak and Jordan watered the growing plant. Finally, I am ready to harvest the tree's fruits for the benefit of the world.

Old pirates, yes, they rob I,
Sold I to the merchant ships,
Minutes after they took I
From the bottomless pit.
But my 'and was made strong
By the 'and of the Almighty.
We forward in this generation
Triumphantly.
Bob Marley, "Redemption Song"

TABLE OF CONTENTS

ILLUSTRATIONS

INTRODUCTION

*A*FRIKA'S *STRUGGLE* DEALS with the direct descendant of an African emperor, who was captured and transported to the Americas as a slave. On his journey to freedom, he was educated via his relationship with a German-born plantation owner/adopted father in the Province of Georgia; an English-born abolitionist in New York City; a French intellectual of revolutionary leanings in Montreal, Canada, and renowned institutions in France and in England.

Afrika played a major role in the American Revolution, the French Revolution, and the Haitian Revolution. He negotiated with and fought luminaries of the French Revolution and Napoleonic France. The lessons Afrika learned in regard to the history and philosophy of the West in his education (nurture) and his African imperial lineage (nature) shaped his life and vision of a greater Africa. For example, he believed the Haitian Revolution should be the springboard to an African empire similar to the way the French Revolution had been the springboard to the Napoleonic French Empire with its ambitions to rule the world. Afrika preferred a Greater Africa ruled by an emperor (e.g., a Napoleonic figure) rather than a republic ruled by a president (e.g., a Washingtonian figure). He admired the nationalistic and presocialist (the forerunner to the socialism of today) ideals embraced by the French and other European liberals and radicals.

Afrika's Struggle takes on the double meaning of Africa the land and Afrika the man—Afrika enslaved yet educated by Western civilization, which taught him how to aspire to become a master of his environment by its philosophy and its history.

PART ONE

IN THE BEGINNING

Look to Africa, for there a king will be crowned.

— MARCUS MOSIAH GARVEY

1

THE UNKNOWN BETRAYAL OF
MY RAVENOUS KINSMAN

I FIRST BECAME suspicious when I heard the strange noises in the night—the trotting of feet through the kraal. Plus, I heard camouflaging calls and whispering sounds that were similar to the Nekjonian warriors' vocal style.

For many generations, our kingdom, Orego, had been in conflict with the neighboring kingdom, Nekjo. The two kingdoms had once formed a great empire, Kenjo, in the inland region. The empire was controlled by a powerful but benevolent *huii-ahj* (huii, the official/high rank; and ahj, the ruler/emperor), Orego-ahj. His empire was a vast area covering the Kilatan Plain—the largest plain in the region. Prior to his rule, most of the tribal territories on the outskirts of the empire had been conquered. In fact, the already-conquered territories made the kingdom into an empire. The members of these tribes had to pay tributes and were coercively governed by the Kenjonian laws, customs and traditions. In addition, they had to speak the Kenjonian language and wear Kenjonian clothing. They were subjects under the empire of Kenjo but never received the privileges of Kenjonian citizens. This subjugation caused many uprisings and rebellions from the conquered tribes, even unto the end of Orego-ahj rule, but their retaliations were subdued by the powerful Kenjonian army and the Imperial Guard (Orego-ahj's personal bodyguards).

Orego-ahj had thirteen wives and many concubines. His first wife, Nakota-ahjess, was his favorite wife. He loved her amorously and made her his queen. She bore him two sons—twins. He named the firstborn Orego, which means powerful and kind natured. He named the second Nekjo, which is derived from Kenjo (the kingdom), meaning powerful and dominant. Orego-ahj's other wives and concubines bore him children who were below the status of the firstborn twin.

Orego and Nekjo were grown young men. They were handsome, tall, black, and strong. Their lean and ripped physiques glistened like polished bronze. Orego-ahj, advanced in age, had to decide who would be his successor to the throne. According to protocol, the firstborn son should be the successor upon Orego-ahj's death. Therefore, Orego-ahj preferred Orego (especially Orego's favorable traits) to Nekjo. The latter perceived his father's favoritism—which kindled Nekjo's heart with jealousy. In everything, he tried to grudgingly compete against his brother. In the Kenjonian army, Orego was the huii of the spearmen and machete men (swordsmen). He was assigned to make peace treaties and negotiations with neighboring kingdoms and tribes. Nekjo was the huii of the archers, and he was assigned to invent and carry out war strategies against neighboring tribes and kingdoms. In addition, in the kingdom, Orego was the chief huii of the body of huiis who made the laws for the citizens and conquered tribes. He was the chief justice who interpreted the laws, customs, and traditions. Nekjo was the top huii of the body of huiis who enforced the laws, customs, and traditions. Both Orego and Nekjo reported to their father about any decisions concerning the kingdom and its army.

Increasingly, Nekjo envied his brother, especially for his higher positions and authority in the kingdom and its army. Orego-ahj perceived Nekjo's jealousy and grudge, but he did not do anything except continue his observation. On his deathbed, he called his two sons and said, "Orego and Nekjo, my sons, I will be joining my ancestors. So there will be a huii-ahj ceremony and a great feast on the next moon. According to tradition, the firstborn will be my successor. During the ceremony, Orego will choose thirteen virgins to be his wives." As his father continued, Nekjo swallowed his spittle as if it were a lump of gall, although he knew that his brother's succession was inevitable. In acquiescence,

Orego discreetly smiled and bowed as he walked backward from his father's presence.

This was the moon (day) of the great huii-ahj ceremony. There was laughter and a joyous atmosphere in the cavernous courtrooms and courtyards. Moreover, there was a large variety of food such as yams, herbs, meat, alcohol, and others. Furthermore, the huii-ahj, huiis, and invited dignitaries from nearby and faraway kingdoms and tribes attended the imperial ceremony. Toward the end of the ceremony, Orego-ahj crowned Orego with the imperial headdress, which was made from ostrich feathers. Next, he clothed him with the royal robe, which was made from leopard skins. Afterward, he gave him the imperial scepter, which was made of carved and polished mahogany adorned with gold and diamonds. The hair of a giraffe's tail protruded from the end of the scepter. Then he gave Orego the bejeweled imperial amulet and golden ring. Finally, the high priest gave him the imperial liquor mingled with lion blood, which Orego drank as an oath to his subjects to show that he was the new huii-ahj of the empire of Kenjo—a huii-ahj who would govern under the rule of law set forth by ancestral customs and traditions. Acquiescently, he bowed to his father and was granted the golden and bejeweled imperial throne stylized with lion carvings. It was a gigantic chair with a headrest, armrests, and a footstool of fur coverings. In response, the citizens and foreigners gave Orego a standing ovation and shouted, "Hail to the new huii-ahj of Kenjo! May the gods and ancestors bless your seed so that your dynasty will rule the world for eternity! Long live Orego and your everlasting empire. Hail! Hail! Hail!" Furiously, Huii Nekjo shrugged his shoulders and beckoned to his servants to follow him out of the courts. When he passed the arched columns, he saw Natika, one of the virgins chosen by his brother for a wife. Disappointedly, he stared at her as he slowly moved his gaze to his brother. In retaliation, Huii Orego (now Orego-ahj) sternly stared at him. Like his brother, Huii Nekjo admired Nakita very much. In addition, he understood that by law, a virgin chosen and bought by a man cannot marry or be bought by another man, even after the groom's death.

On the moon after the huii-ahj ceremony, Orego-ahj's father called him unto his chambers. He started, "My son, you are the huii-ahj of Kenjo now. Rule our people according to our ancestral customs, traditions, and laws. Moreover, you are wise…be aware of your brother's ambition."

Respectfully, Orego-ahj exited his father's quarters as he pondered his father's statements. A few moons later, Orego-ahj's father died. His body was consumed with his wives and personal possessions in a bonfire.

Now Orego-ahj was the huii-ahj of Kenjo. He tried to rule the vast empire according to the teachings of his father and tutors. Howbeit, he abided by his own philosophy like his many predecessors. Constantly, Orego-ahj realized his brother's recalcitrance. Fearing that his brother would overthrow or murder him if Huii Nekjo were to receive Orego-ahj's former titles, positions, and authority, Orego-ahj gave them to his youngest maternal uncle instead.

Recognizing the slight, Huii Nekjo demanded that the Imperial Guard allow him to see Orego-ahj. Orego-ahj permitted his request. Huii Nekjo strode toward the huii-ahj and acquiescently bowed. He immediately rebounded, "Hail! O Great Huii-ahj. Why are you harshly mistreating your brother and humble servant?" Huii Nekjo paused and earnestly listened for his brother to reply.

"Because of your perfidious ambition to seize my throne," replied Orego-ahj.

"Hail! O Great Huii-ahj. On what grounds do you base your judgment?" asked Huii Nekjo.

"On many grounds that I will not address with you at this time!" answered Orego-ahj. "Ahem! Due to my leniency, I will not exile or imprison you. Sad to say, you wouldn't show me such mercy if our roles were reversed," continued Orego-ahj. "Nope, you would have done worse to me and my household. Anyway, I deprived you of my former titles, power, and authority, which is a greater punishment than exile or imprisonment," stated Orego-ahj. "Now get out of my sight! By the way, consider what remains of your power and authority to be probationary until further notice!" exclaimed Orego-ahj.

Huii Nekjo pierced the eyes of the huii-ahj with his gaze as he quietly bowed and backwardly exited.

In fear for his life, the huii-ahj strengthened his Imperial Guard. He had Huii Marko (his best friend and chief of the Imperial Guard) increase his bodyguard detail, stationed more Imperial Guard within and around the palaces, sent spies to shadow Huii Nekjo's movements, and bribed some of Huii Nekjo's closest associates for information.

In the interim, Huii Nekjo secretly tried to persuade most of the men under his command and the citizens of the western region of the empire in his favor. He persuaded most of the citizens of the west, along with his men, who were called Uncotomos (right-wing conservatives and fanatical zealots of an expanding Greater Kenjonian Empire). There were many reasons why Huii Nekjo was successful. First, the western regions were rugged, less fertile, and near the jungle. The palace was situated in the center of the kingdom, closer to the eastern region, which was composed mostly of the fertile Kilatan plain and rich farmlands. Second, most of the huiis were chosen from the eastern region. The citizens of the western region were more heavily taxed than those in the eastern lands because most of the conquered tribal territories that were also giving tributes were located on the outskirts of the eastern region. Third, Huii Nekjo was the top huii in the western region, and he was the huii-ahj's twin. Due to his sphere of influence, western citizens believed that if they placed their trust in him, he would use his imperial connections to persuade the huii-ahj on their behalf. Finally, the information that Orego-ahj received from his spies was not concrete enough to accuse Huii Nekjo justly on any grounds. Furthermore, the majority of the bribed colleagues of Nekjo were Uncotomos who took money from the huii-ahj and gave him false reports. Huii Nekjo was very strong and influential in the western region of the kingdom and in the army (mostly with the archers), and that would enable him to start a revolution if the huii-ahj should loosen his grip on the empire. At the time, the empire was like a pot of boiling water gathering enough steam pressure to capsize the cover.

Many moons after the inauguration of Orego-ahj, he held a meeting with Huii Nago (his maternal uncle) and the body of huiis, excluding Huii Nekjo and his overt loyalists (who supported the politics of the Uncotomos). At the assembly, he discussed his decision to grant independence to Klye and Hyu, two tribes of the conquered tribal territories, as a reward for their consistent loyalty to the empire. (In reverse psychology, he wanted to use the two tribes as examples to mollify the rest of the restless empire.)

"Hail! O Great Huii-ahj! I think you should reconsider your decision because independence would motivate a chain of uprisings and revolts in the rest of the tribal territories like in the past, during your father's rule. Yep, as the saying goes, 'Give them a yard, and they will take a mile.' O Great Huii-ahj! They will misconstrue your kindness for weakness and reward your benevolence with violence. Hail!" advised Huii Nago.

"How dare you oppose my decision?" exclaimed Orego-ahj.

Apologetically, Huii Nago shrugged and bowed his head. He knew Orego-Ahj was breaking a traditional rule that opposed the liberation of tribal territories under Kenjonian rule. However, he ended the debate because he did not want to jeopardize his status (officially, he was Huii Nekjo's equal as per the powers given to him by the huii-ahj).

Orego-ahj concluded, "The next two moons, I want you to pass the law ratifying the independence of the two tribes."

"My huii-ahj, we will pass the law. Hail!" agreed the Huiis.

Although they agreed with Huii Nago's argument, they were bound by their oath to obey the absolute rule of the huii-ahj. After all, Orego-ahj was the Kenjonian Empire as the Kenjonian Empire was Orego-ahj. Plus, the majority of the huiis were fanatically loyal to the huii-ahj. Other supporters of Orego-ahj were found in the army (especially the spearmen and machete men). The supporters were later called Naturnos.

By the second moon, the law was passed. Klye and Hyu became independent tribes. They were linked to the empire via social ties and other relationships.

Huii Nekjo and his loyal faction were angry when the law was passed. He wrote an open letter to his brother, protesting, "Hail! O Great Huii-ahj. Why have you broken the invariable laws of our ancestors? Our sacred tradition opposes the granting of autonomy to conquered kingdoms!"

Angrily, Orego-ahj contemplated the punishment for his audacious sibling. The Kenjonians had noticed the daring character of Huii Nekjo. As a matter of fact, Nekjo had developed allegiances among the Imperial Guard, palace courtiers, the priesthood, and most of the Kenjonians in the western region. He was able to maintain their commitment through skillful propaganda and meeting their needs (e.g., providing food for impoverished areas). Therefore, he was unofficially treated as the de facto huii-ahj in the western region. The Uncotomos were not going to allow the Imperial Guard to arrest him without dogged resistance that could escalate into a civil war or, worse, anarchy.

Furthermore, the western Kenjonians supported Huii Nekjo's letter because they feared Orego-ahj would increase their taxes to compensate for the former tributes of Klye and Hyu. Buoyed by popular support, certain Uncotomos declared Huii Nekjo the huii-ahj of Western Kenjo.

Orego-ahj called for an assembly to debate his next step. Under the darkened clouds, he didn't want to make a unilateral decision. Instead, he wanted to gauge the direction he should take via feedback from his assembly. Unfortunately, Orego-ahj's worst fear was confirmed. The assembly, composed of huiis, army officers, priests, and Imperial Guard, pressed him to divide the empire in order to avoid a bloody civil war. Besides, there were hostile independent tribes located on the northern, southern, and eastern frontiers that were preparing to cause trouble during an anarchic civil war. In other words, the empire would fall apart like a broken egg.

The assembly advised the Huii-ahj to convene a summit with his brother to negotiate a settlement—a settlement that would transform the empire into two kingdoms: West Kenjo and East Kenjo.

Reluctantly, Huii Nekjo agreed to the summit because his goal of overthrowing his twin (to rule a united Kenjo Empire) was precluded by many obstacles. First, only a third of the army (mainly archers) supported him. In turn, Orego-ahj has the support of two-thirds of the army and the Imperial Guard. Moreover, Orego-ahj could easily boycott the western region, since the breadbasket was located in the eastern region.

Like a Greek tragedy, the seductive goddess of intrigue is always operating behind the scenes. She is like the puppet master on the fifteenth Tarot card that manipulates humanity with a string without its knowledge. Huii Marko, chief of the Imperial Guard, wanted to maintain the union. He was an ideologue who believed the empire and the Huii-ahj to be one—an entity. If the empire was divided, then the Huii-ahj would be divided. If the empire fell apart, the Huii-ahj would fall apart. Biblically, he agreed that "a house divided against itself cannot stand." He was a fanatical Imperial Guard who thought the empire should strike back against any challenges to its imperial power. At all costs, the union had to be preserved. He would rather commit suicide than to see things fall apart in his beloved Kenjonian Empire.

Huii Marko arranged a secret meeting with the most powerful men of the Naturno faction, excluding Huii Nago (the prime minister/chancellor). He excluded Huii Nago because he was an uncle of Huii Nekjo and he wanted peace at all costs. For example, he was the closest advisor to the Huii-ahj, and he appealed to most of the huiis' fears—the unpredictability and instability a civil war would create for their comfort zones. Worse yet, the rank and file of the empire dreaded the idea of warring against their families and friends in a civil war. After all, the Kenjonian society was a family-oriented society—a clannish society.

He invited Huii Benko, the commander in chief of the imperial army. He was a mentor of Huii Marko. In his youth, Huii Benko was nicknamed the Honey Badger—a fearless and ferocious fighter.

Next, he invited Huii Rodnonko—the chief legislator of the Imperial Legislature. Huii Rodnonko was one of the richest men in the Kenjonian Empire. He represented the interests of the wealthy merchants and their ilk. He realized a divided empire would bring instability in the sphere of politics and commerce. Besides, he knew "war is good" for his wealthy associates and himself. Secretly, they could profit from both parties (the Uncotomos and the Naturnos) during a short war. In the long run, Huii Rodnonko's heart was in the unity of the empire because law and order is conducive to business.

Then he invited Huii Rodbeko—the chief justice of the Imperial Court. Huii Rodbeko was the godfather of Orego-ahj. He was the best friend of the late father of the Huii-ahj. He was a living symbol of the Kenjonian tradition and customs. He was nicknamed the Owl because he had an oval face with big eyes. On the other hand, he was one of the wisest elders of the empire. He was greatly respected for his unrivaled sapience.

Finally, Huii Marko invited Huii Jajordo—the high priest of the Imperial Temple. He was the godfather of Huii Nekjo. He was troubled by a dream he had had a few moons earlier. He had burned sacrifices to his ancestors and to the gods to stave off the omen. He had dreamed that Huii Kenjo (lineage) sold his soul to pale-faced demons in exchange for the empire. Plus, he offered his brother as a burned offering to seal the deal. Ravenously, the pale-faced demons demanded more sacrifices to satisfy their unquenchable thirst for human blood.

Unable to fulfill their quota, Huii Kenjo (his lineage) would allow them to rape, pillage, and plunder the empire like hyenas and vultures ravaging a dying elephant. In his vision, he inspected the skeleton that the scavenging demons had picked clean. In a trance induced by herbs, he communicated with his ancestors and gods. They told him the empire would be divided, but a fiery lion would rise out of the ashes of the empire—a lion that would be able to fly like the demons because they would teach him the art of flying. He would be protected by the ancestors and gods while he was living in their abode. He would be the avenger of Kenjo. He would unite the empire, both on earth and in the sky. The dynasty of Orego-ahj would continue to live through him. Howbeit, Huii Marko (his lineage) would have to offer himself as a sacrifice because he was the symbol of the protection the lion of Kenjo would receive.

Huii Jajordo confided his visions to Huii Marko, using his connection to influence the huii-ahj. The huii-ahj could be stubborn and aloof, whereas others were afraid to approach him with bad news or uncomfortable views. In turn, Huii Marko—a man of practical and secular bearings—realized he could use the high priest's visions to good propaganda effect.

Huii Marko used the secret meeting to get the powerful men on the same page as they searched to find a final solution to the Nekjonian problem. He played upon their fanatic loyalty to the huii-ahj as well as their own self-interest. Finally, they endorsed Huii Marko's idea of using a secret weapon to get Orego-ahj's undivided attention and unwavering commitment to their objectives. He decided to use his half sister and the most favorite wife of the Huii-ahj—the most beautiful woman of the Kenjonian Empire—Empress Nakita-ahjess.

Huii Marko invited his half sister Empress Nakita-ahjess to his country home. He impressed upon the empress that she was needed by the gods and ancestors to save the empire. In turn, she would be able to save Orego-ahj and her children's future. He revealed Huii Jajordo's vision to her. He continued, "Operation One Empire will be a surgical strike based on intricate planning that will need precise execution. Therefore, I am going to provide you with a vision that you will convey to your husband. He has to believe that you dreamed the vision, and he must not see my involvement. In turn, he is going to contact the high priest for its interpretation. The high priest will be able to convince him of the foreboding omen. Then Orego-ahj will turn to his advisors in the Imperial Guard, imperial army, and the legislative and judicial bodies. In unison, we will counsel him to adopt Operation One Empire. Thus, he will change his mind and give us our war."

She was intrigued. "What is the vision?"

He pounced. "After you make love to our beloved Huii-ahj, you'll appear to be distressed and frightened. In concern, he will ask you about your problem. Tell him you are worried about a vision you dreamed. In the vision, you saw two male lions ruling a pride. There was a disturbance in the bush. The male lions went to investigate the commotion. Apparently, they ran into a lion hunter. The hunter threw his spear and fatally wounded the elder lion. As per tradition, the unharmed younger lion should have pounced, revengefully, on the unarmed hunter, whose spear was stuck in the wounded elder lion. Instead, the younger lion covetously returned to the pride to kill the offspring of the elder lion and to mate with the wives of his dying elder brother, to produce his own offspring.

"The lion hunter completed his killing and freed his spear from the carcass of the elder lion, and he was able to kill the younger lion because he was alone. The pride, without a male protector, became easy prey to the clever hunter, hyenas, and the malevolent elements of the jungle. If the younger lion had pounced on the unarmed hunter, he would have killed the future killer of the pride and himself. Thus, the pride would have lived forever."

Empress Nakita-ahjess was impressed with the intelligence of her half brother. He bid her good-bye and gave her the Orego-ahj salute (which was similar to the Roman salute to Caesar).

As expected, Orego-ahj bought the deception, or, better yet, the change of direction. He reversed his decision and decided to implement Operation One Empire. Huii Nako protested and threatened to resign. Orego-ahj ordered Huii Nako to withdraw his resignation. He proceeded, "Huii Nako, my uncle, the huii-ahj needs you. The empire needs you. We have to be united in our gravest hour. We have to be united for the empire. We have to be united for the huii-ahj. As a matter of fact, Huii Marko and Huii Benko will be reporting to us on the progress of the war. You and I will be the top two commanders of the campaign."

Huii Nako replied, "My huii-ahj, I am second to none in my loyalty to you. I will obey your command. I will give you my unwavering commitment. Now I will attend to my duty to sell our civil war to the populace. We will win! Hail! Hail! Hail!"

Huii Nekjo's effective intelligence informed him about Operation One Empire. He realized the only option he possessed to retain his power was to declare a civil war. He hoped to separate the empire into two kingdoms, and, maybe on a moon to come, his kingdom may conquer and reunite the kingdoms under his regime. Unfortunately, Huii Nekjo's strategy turned out to be a betrayal instead of a road to unity.

On the fifteenth moon after the two tribes' independence, the civil war began. The empire was divided into two camps. The Uncotomos, mostly from the western region, were supporters of Huii Nekjo. The Naturnos, mostly from the eastern region, were supporters of the huii-ahj. Orego-ahj sent half of his Imperial Guard and army to subdue Huii Nekjo and his forces. In turn, Huii Nekjo and his army set up barricades and waited for his opponents. Huii Nekjo was planning to fight a defensive war. Orego-ahj faced many disadvantages that made it difficult for him to subdue Huii Nekjo and his followers. Firstly, conquered tribal territories were on the outskirts of the eastern region. When the civil war was declared, most of them saw the chance to totally separate from the empire. They gained their independence by fighting the eastern Kenjonians. Thus, Orego-ahj had to fight a two-front war: Huii Nekjo on the Western Front and the revolting tribes on the Eastern Front. Secondly, the tribes of Klye and Hyu aided the huii-ahj against Huii Nekjo, but they did not campaign against the tribal rebellions. In their view, the breakaway tribes were fighting for a just cause—liberation. Thirdly, a few of the conquered tribes (the weaker ones) nomadically deserted the empire, while others remained neutral in the civil war. They, too, peacefully gained their independence. Fourthly, the two-front war placed a strain on logistics and manpower. For example, Orego-ahj had to exhaust his reserves because some of the imperial soldiers switched to their tribal or political allegiances. He had to retain a standing army around the palace and capitol. Plus, he had to divide his forces between the Western Front and the Eastern Front. Therefore, he was unable to meet his brother on the battlefield with a full force. Fifthly, the Uncotomos were mostly archers and hunters who were renowned for their skill and stealth. They built barricades around them from which they shot their arrows at the Naturnos. Although the latter carried shields, most of them were unable to get in at a close range where they could utilize their spears and machetes. Instead, they were forced to retreat to the eastern regions. In addition, their disadvantages were compounded when Huii Nekjo's able commanders (I will discuss them later) introduced deadlier forms of warfare: poison arrows (tipped in the venom of cobras and puff adders), fiery arrows (to burn wooden defenses), burning stones (stones wrapped in burning grass/hay/fuel, which are rolled down steep terrain, from high ground, into Orego-ahj's military formations on the plain), and other innovative arts of war.

Incredibly, a few Naturnos were able to bypass the flying arrows and barricades, but they were outnumbered behind the enemy's line. Others were unfamiliar with the eastern terrain; thus, they were easily ambushed by Huii Nekjo's forces. A few tried to escape via the jungle, but they were attacked by wild animals after getting lost. Still others were cut off from their supplies and units. These soldiers were killed by the "take no prisoner" policy of the able but ruthless commanders of Huii Nekjo. (On the other hand, some soldiers were taken prisoner to be used as bargain chips in later negotiations.)

Finally, Huii Nekjo was more experienced and ingenious in war strategies and military techniques than Orego-ahj and Huii Nago. Innately, Orego-ahj and Huii Nago were of a diplomatic character, which was compounded by their respective training in diplomatic affairs. They placed two able commanders, Huii Marko and Huii Benko, on a short leash. Huii Nago stifled the competent commanders' brilliant ideas. He tweaked their ingenious plan to conduct the war by not following Operation One Empire to the letter. Huii Nago's position as the prime minister (and chief of staff to the Huii-ahj) frustrated their attempts to contact Orego-ahj. Huii Nago would pull rank over the commanders. Orego-ahj became very paranoid and sank into a bunker mentality. He trusted Huii Nago to enter his new constricted world as the empire collapsed around him. He began to blame Huii Marko, Huii Benko, and the other hawks for his dilemma (at the behest of Huii Nago). Ironically, Huii Marko and Huii Benko were talented executives who could have earned the final victory if they had not been harnessed by Orego-ahj and Huii Nago.

On the other hand, Huii Nekjo gave a blank check to his most able commanders, Huii Darko and Huii Killa. Huii Darko was an ingenious, eloquent, elegant, and charismatic warrior who was renowned for his disarming smile. He was nicknamed the Leopard because of his stealth and agility. Huii Darko was tall, dark, and handsome. He had perfect symmetry in his facial features, which made him the handsomest man in Kenjo—a beauty that facilitated many romantic affairs, which led to many duels.

Huii Darko was named after the Kenjonian god of intelligence (similar to the Greek god Hermes). Boastingly, he would remark that his father was not his biological father. He claimed his mother (whom he loved very much) copulated with Darko (god of intelligence), a copulation that produced a demigod—him, Darko the Great.

The darker side of Huii Darko was disguised under his brighter façade. Underneath, he was a ruthless psychopath. Always, he maintained he wasn't an ideologue like Huii Killa, but he was a revolutionary. He was drawn to Huii Nekjo's rebellion because of its revolutionary attributes. In actuality, Huii Darko was respected as Huii Nekjo's brain, while Huii Killa was called Huii Nekjo's brawn.

Huii Nekjo's brawn was nicknamed the Rhino. Huii Killa (named after the Kilatan Plain) was a vocal and a burly warrior. He was celebrated as the strongest man in the empire. Importantly, he was a childhood friend of Huii Nekjo. He and Huii Darko were allowed to deliver for their team the victory that escaped their counterparts—Huii Marko and Huii Benko—due to their strangulation by Orego-ahj and his chancellor.

Within thirteen moons, the civil war was over. Thirteen thousand men were killed, and twice that were wounded. The western Kenjonians and the former conquered tribal territories gained their independence. (The water had boiled over, and the lid had blown off.) Orego-ahj was the ruler of the eastern Kenjonians, and Huii Nekjo was the ruler of the western Kenjonians.

A few moons after the civil war, the divided empire signed many peace and land treaties. The western Kenjonians received the western region of the former empire and part of the Kilatan Plain, and the eastern Kenjonians received the eastern region of the empire and part of the Kilatan Plain. The tribal territories received the lands they had had before they were conquered, and beyond the outskirts of the former empire.

Orego-ahj and his brother named their respective kingdoms after themselves. As before, Huii Nekjo continued to hope that one day his new, militant kingdom would reunite the kingdom of Orego by force. Meanwhile, Orego hoped that his kingdom would reunite with his brother's kingdom via diplomatic means. After their respective deaths, coincidentally, the kingdoms devolved into separate tribes, which were the most powerful tribes in the tribal territories—the golden era of the empire degenerated into an era of iron and clay (tribalism), from an emperor of an august empire to petty chieftains of tribes. In Nekjo, the sons of Huii Nekjo had the same traits as their father. Supported by certain huiis, the younger sons verbally revolted against the eldest son, who was not capable of controlling them. In order to prevent a civil war, the huiis of the new kingdom agreed to rule it equally among themselves (a senate presided over by a chieftain). Each huii represented the interests of a certain region of the tribe. Likewise, the kingdom of Orego adopted the political changes of her neighbor because of similar challenges.

The preceding is the history of our tribe, Orego, and our neighboring tribe, Nekjo.

Many generations after the civil war, our tribe continued to be in conflict with our neighboring tribe, Nekjo. The Nekjonians were our principal rival in the tribal territories. Although the Oregonians had very strong, skillful, trained, and well-organized warriors, we were vulnerable to the Nekjonians' advanced archery and ruthless plundering. Thus, the two evenly matched tribes cautiously watched each other without leaping into open warfare. However, the Nekjonians declared war on smaller and weaker tribes for various political reasons. Other tribes would seek protection via alliances with Orego. In turn, Orego would offer to form alliances with the preceding tribes to check Kenjo's expansion and power.

Smaller and weaker tribes wishing to remain neutral between the two great tribal powers approached Orego (the lesser of two evils) to intervene and to propose a peace treaty within the tribal territories. The Oregonian huiis agreed and proposed intertribal laws. Surprisingly, the Nekjonians agreed to the peace treaty for a short period of time. In fact, they agreed because they weren't in a position to guarantee victory in a showdown between them and us. Besides, the peace treaty did not provide a strong enforcement—it didn't have teeth. The treaty provided for limited sanctions, diplomatic isolation, and a threat of war—a war that would negatively impact everyone.

A few moons after the intertribal law was passed, there were various rumors about strange beings traveling on multiwinged great canoes appearing out of the unknown—from the great beyond—from the edges of the earth. There were added rumors that their presence caused tensions and turmoil in the coastal kingdoms and tribal territories. The rumors became more shocking when the tribes in our tribal territories learned that the strange beings had arrived into Nekjo.

A few moons after the arrival of the strange beings in Nekjo, Nekjo returned to plunder her smaller and weaker neighboring tribes. She had broken the intertribal peace treaty that regulated open warfare and banned plundering. In their battles, Nekjonians were utilizing iron rods that shot lightning with a sound of thunder. The Oregonians learned that the Nekjonians exchanged captives from the conquered tribes to the strange beings for iron rods and other goods.

All the other tribes who were parties to the intertribal treaty appealed to Orego to organize a war campaign against Nekjo and the strange beings. In turn, the huiis of Orego convened an assembly to debate a declaration of war. Huii Muraso was the Oregonian chieftain who presided over the body of huiis. He was the direct descendant of the former Orego-ahj of Kenjo. Huii Crawfo was the most powerful huii under the chieftain and his best friend. Coincidentally, he was the direct descendant of the legendary Huii Marko—the chief of the Imperial Guard of Kenjo and its huii-ahj.

Importantly, Huii Crawfo was the chief of the Black Panther Society—an ultra-right-wing (conservative), secret society started by Huii Marko and Huii Jajordo (high priest of the Imperial Temple).

After Orego-ahj failed to repress the revolt of his brother, ultraconservative huiis lost faith in him—especially in the division of their beloved empire. At the behest of Huii Jajordo, Huii Marko formed a secret society centered on the vision/prophecy of Huii Jajordo. According to Huii Jajordo's prophecy, he was troubled by a dream. He burned sacrifices to his ancestors and to the gods to stave off the omen. He dreamed Huii Kenjo (lineage) sold his soul to pale-faced demons in exchange for the empire. Plus, he offered his brother (lineage) as a burned offering to seal the deal. Ravenously, the pale-face demons demanded more sacrifices to satisfy their unquenchable thirst for human blood. Unable to fulfill their quota, Huii Kenjo (lineage) would allow them to rape, pillage, and plunder the empire like hyenas and vultures ravaging a dying elephant. In his vision, he inspected the skeleton that the scavenging demons had picked clean. In a trance induced by herbs, he communicated with his ancestors and gods. They told him the empire would be divided, but a fiery lion would rise out of the ashes of the empire—a lion that would be able to fly like the demons because they would teach him the art of flying. (It would be like a wasp planting her larvae in a caterpillar, developing into a full-grown wasp emerging from the caterpillar's carcass). He would be protected by the ancestors and gods while living in their abode. He would be the avenger of Kenjo. He would unite the empire, both on earth and in the sky. The dynasty of Orego-ahj would continue to live through him. Howbeit, Huii Marko (lineage) would have to offer himself as a sacrifice because he was the symbol of the protection the lion of Kenjo would receive.

Huii Marko named the secret society the Black Panther because of its secrecy, stealth, and other phantomlike and nocturnal attributes (e.g., the black panther/leopard is known as a creature of the night). In addition, he selected initiates from the former Imperial Guard (later, initiates were selected at the age of thirteen from across the social spectrum of Oregonian society). The initiates were sworn to secrecy on the penalty of death. They had to be of pure blood (unblemished), with ancestry that could be traced to the Kenjonian Empire. He shifted their allegiance from King Orego to the rebirth of a reunited empire and the birth of "the fiery lion"—the future emperor—the Kenjonian messiah (according to Huii Jajordo's prophecy). The initiates were tattooed (carved) under their right arm with the Kenjonian character for the number thirteen. Thirteen was a lucky number in the Kenjonian religion. According to the prophecy, "the Kenjonian messiah will have a birthmark denoting the character for the number thirteen under his right arm." Moreover, the initiates were trained in the martial arts and voodoo (similar to Animism and Totemism evolving into a Caribbean religion based on a mix of African and Christian elements). In fact, they were the most skilled warriors and priests—warrior-priests sworn to "death before surrender," similar to the early Knights Templar and the early Teutonic Knights.

Huii Crawfo was the leader and product of the secretive Black Panther Society, which had existed for many generations. During the war council, Chieftain Muraso directed Huii Crawfo to bring the council to a close. Huii Crawfo concluded, "Gentlemen, we outnumber our enemies ten to one. In turn, they have strange weapons and strange allies who speak like the wildebeests. I'm confident our forces will be able to defeat them on the field of battle. If not, we will fight to the death." The following moon, an entourage was dispatched to Nekjo with a declaration of war. Nekjo agreed to the terms of engagement and the battlefield. Hence, the war was set to take place on the Kilatan Plain on the fifth moon.

Nekjo knew of the superior quantity (including Orego's allies) and the quality of the strong, skillful, trained, and well-organized warriors of Orego. In spite of their advanced archery and exotic weapons, Nekjo didn't want to risk open warfare. Instead, they secretly planned a surprise attack on Orego, which would be followed by ruthless plundering. Furthermore, Nekjo knew that Orego's demise would cause the other tribes to hopelessly surrender without a fight. The other option for the other clans would be to flee to other tribal territories. Unfortunately, the fleeing ethnic groups would encounter resistance from tribes already residing in those territories. Therefore, they would be "jumping out of the frying pan into the fire."

Plus, Kenjo received strategic advice from the strange beings—Portuguese slave traders. During the war council, Captain Ben Alvarez and his first officer, David Cardoso, advised the Nekjonian chieftain via a translator. Captain Alvarez counseled Chieftain Fogo, a direct descendant of Huii Nekjo, "You must raid Orego under the cover of darkness. Aren't they going to have a moon festival or some crap of that sort…? Like a clan of hyenas, if you kill the alpha female, Orego, then the rest—the other tribes—will run away."

First Officer David Cardoso continued, "As a matter of fact, the festival will occur on the night of a full moon. Our forces will have the moonlight and the torches to assist us during our surprise raid."

Chieftain Fogo agreed. "Well, gentlemen, we will attack Orego during the festival of the moon goddess, Setina. Are there any objections? If not, we'll execute our plan during the early dawn following the festival. Gentlemen, we have our war and the opportunity to unite our empire in memory of our ancestor King Kenjo. We will call the war campaign Operation One Empire II."

At the other camp, Oregonian huiis wisely debated the need to post sentries around the kraals after spies tipped off Oregonian intelligence of a possible surprise attack. Unfortunately, the spies didn't know on which moon it would occur. Moreover, Orego didn't expect a nocturnal attack because wars, historically, were never fought during the night or on holidays. Nevertheless, the Portuguese slave traders "rewrote the Kenjonian pamphlet" on the art of war by introducing new Western martial arts. Let's not forget, the Nekjonians wanted to reunite an empire, while the Europeans wanted slaves (captives of the nocturnal raid) to increase their wealth. After the debate, Orego and the other tribes posted sentries around the borders of the kraals.

On the eve of the fourth moon, Orego and her allies had a great feast. They performed rituals and danced the Sacred War Dance (as per Kenjonian tradition, in which a dance would be held before open warfare). Only men were allowed to perform and to attend the sacred dance. The children and women stayed in their huts. After the sacred occasion, most of the men were drunk and filled. The sentries were not accustomed to having a constant watch. They fell asleep at their posts. Culturally, the Nekjonians were aware of the lack of vigilance of their enemy. Ruthlessly, they set their operation in motion.

Now it started to happen—the Nekjonians carried out their surprise attack on our village. I heard the screaming and wailing of the women and the children, as well as the crackling sounds of the huts as the fire hungrily consumed them. I heard the war cries of the Nekjonians and the distressed cries of my people. Furthermore, I heard sounds likened unto thunder while I saw flashes of lightning against the fabric of the nocturnal sky. I started to cry and ran into my mother's arms for refuge. The kraals were in turmoil. A tall Nekjonian warrior burst through the curtain at the door and held on to my mama. I hollered, kicked, and bit the man to let my mama go. In retaliation, he swung his arm toward my head.

On the next moon, I found myself chained by my neck, ankles, and wrists to a group of children. I felt a clot of blood on my head and a terrible headache. Next, I looked around, mostly with the intention of finding my mama—she was nowhere to be found. There were young men, women, and children in chains and fetters—the spoils of war. For the first time, I saw the strange beings accompanied by Nekjonian warriors. The colors of their skin contrasted with one another against the rising sun as the morning fog turned into a drizzle—as if the gods and the ancestors were weeping. Once again, I turned to look for Mama, but I only saw in the distance the swirling gray smoke of the massacre of the kraals of our tribe as the Nekjonians and the strange beings led us to an unknown destination.

Slave Caravans on the Road

Source: *"Africans in America"* located on the website below -
http://www.pbs.org/wgbh/aia/part1/1h321b.html

2

In the Belly of the Beast

Like a herd of cattle, we were led on a thirteen-day march to the coastline. During the march, we lost a few slaves who were whipped to keep pace. If they still failed to keep up, the Portuguese slave drivers would club them to death with their iron rods (guns). They preferred to save their ammunition for slave hunting.

When we arrived at the coastline, I was awed at the multiwinged canoes (slave ships) that had been rumored in Orego. Like a marketplace consumer differentiating between the good fruits and the bad fruits, the Portuguese sailors would select the able-bodied Africans from the rest of the captives. Captives who were not selected were left to die or were killed on the shores. I was fettered to Huii Crawfo after the selection process. I was surprised to see a powerful warrior shackled to me. Huii Crawfo told me I should be calm because he had been sent to give me hope. He began to unravel the history of our people to me.

During the raid, Huii Crawfo and the chieftain realized that everything was lost. Mercifully, Huii Crawfo killed his family and helped the chieftain to kill his family so that they would not be humiliated as captives of the Nekjonians, especially with rumors expressing that tortured captives were offered as sacrifices to the Europeans. Before the chieftain committed suicide, he gave Huii Crawfo one last order—to kill a son, a love child. Kenjonian honor dictated that a leader should commit suicide with his family to avoid the dishonor of captivity. Huii Crawfo—a Black Panther—obeyed his final order. He escaped the Oregonian debacle by hiding in the jungle. From the canopy of the trees, he observed the chieftain's son taken away with the other captives. He stealthily shadowed the train of slaves to the slave ships. He lived off the land. He took quick naps after the train stopped for food and short breaks. (The Portuguese merchants had to protect their stolen assets.)

During a nap, Kenjonian gods and Huii Crawfo's ancestors appeared to him in a dream. They overrode the late chieftain's order to kill his love child (the chieftain's eldest son) because he was the chosen messiah—the prophesied emperor of the Kenjonian Empire. They continued, "If you look under his right arm, you'll find the birthmark of the Black Panther—the character of the lucky number thirteen. Therefore, we want you to go to the lad and tell him we will protect him on his journey to his destiny. According to your sworn oath as a Black Panther, you may take your life afterward. Thus, you will fulfill the Kenjonian prophecy: 'Huii Marko (lineage) will have to offer himself as a sacrifice to us because he is the symbol of the protection the lion of Kenjo will receive from us.' You are the direct descendant of Huii Marko, and the love child, Kenjo, is the direct descendant of Orego-ahj—emperor of Kenjo." Awakened, Huii Crawfo swore to perform his new duty.

At the coastline, he slipped into the line of slaves during the selection process. He maneuvered to my side. He lifted my right arm to observe my birthmark. I was the one.

By nightfall, we were packed into a ship like fishes packed into a successful fisherman's boat. Huii Crawfo observed the patterns of the sailors. For many days and nights, he keenly studied the operation as he mentally probed for weak points and opportunities. Like a man possessed, he waited for his chance to strike.

In the interim, we were poorly fed. Most times, we had to urinate and defecate where we were chained. At times, they would throw sea water to wash us off. People became sick. The dead were thrown overboard. Most of the sailors whipped the men, played humiliating games with the children, and raped the young women. One day, an enraged Captain Ben Alvarez intervened. "You fucking bastards! You're cutting into my profits by unnecessarily damaging the goods. You fuckers have killed four monkeys and violently raped nineteen—no, twenty—heifers over a period of just five fucking days! Sons of bitches, I dare any of you to kill or severely injure any more of my investments without a just cause. And I'll see to it that you work off the value of the dead or fatally wounded slaves. I have to answer to shareholders and investors about their return on their investments. Smarten up, shape up, or be shipped out! Misshapen dicks! Dave, order some of the fellows to throw this shark food overboard, and notify the clerk to log the losses for insurance purposes. Lie on the causes of death, and tell one of the boys to grab me a flask of rum—Jamaican white rum!"

"Aye, aye, captain!" responded First Officer Cardoso.

Days turned into weeks, and I continued to suffer from the pungent stench, stifling heat, cramped space (under the deck), damp wooden floors, and the excruciating din caused by the agony of my neighbors. Finally, Huii Crawfo revealed his brilliant scheme to me. During the night, he was able to play around with his lock on his wrist by using a wooden splinter and a piece of wire. Carelessly, the guards would fall asleep after they became intoxicated on rum. Methodically, he sprang his shackles and swooped onto a nearby guard with a catlike agility. He silently slit his throat while covering his mouth. He retrieved the dead man's keys and set free most of the men. Awakened from their drunken stupor, the slave pirates tried to fight back, but it was too late. Huii Crawfo sought out the most prolific rapist among them and flogged him with a sharpened pole longer than the poor fellow. Vlad the Impaler would have been proud of Huii Crawfo's work. Like a roasted pig, the pole was rammed through his anus and exited out of his mouth with the assistance of two Negroes.

Beholding the morbid masterpiece of Huii Crawfo, First Officer Cardoso exclaimed, "Oh my...! You are a fucking demon! Who the fuck are you? Die, you piece of shit!" He raised his pistol, squeezed the trigger, and shot Huii Crawfo in the back. As Huii Crawfo stumbled overboard, he shouted to me, "I have done my duty! Kenjo, meet your destiny! May the gods and the ancestors protect you!" He splashed into the inky sea. The Oregonians and others were emboldened by Huii Crawfo's martyrdom and message. (They did not know my name was Kenjo, and they thought he was speaking to them as Kenjonians—perhaps he was speaking to them and me in a double entendre sort of way).

Quickly, they corralled First Officer Cardoso. Stubbornly, he fought to his last round. Fearing he might be impaled like a roast duck, he tried to shoot himself with his last bullet. The pistol jammed. Roco, an Oregonian butcher, placed a knife to his throat. Across the ship, the captain furiously fought with his former captives. He had a pistol in one hand and a cutlass in the other. Realizing the capture of his first officer, he quickly threw away his cutlass and scooped me (I was seven years old) into his arm. He told Roco he was going to shoot me if he didn't release Dave and ordered the Negroes to cease their mutiny. Roco stared at him as he slowly slit Senor Cardoso's throat. The first officer's throat whistled a song as he tried to gasp for breath. It was very eerie. I kept a stoic composure with the knowledge that I was a direct descendant of an emperor destined by the gods and my ancestors to be the future of the empire. Albeit, my pedigree was not known to the other mutineers because Huii Crawfo had not revealed that I was the bearer of the special birthmark foretold by Kenjonian prophecy. Thus, Roco saw me as dispensable in comparison to the lives of the others—a tree in a large forest.

Captain Alvarez realized that he had to think very fast because he risked joining his late, loyal lieutenant wherever slave traders migrated to for an everlasting voyage. The captain beckoned a translator to translate his message. He began, "OK! You win! What do you want me to do? You need me and my men to sail the ship because you won't be able to do so. You have to know how to operate the ship and to navigate by the stars and the instruments. You are doomed without our specialized knowledge. You may run into other hostile ships. There are many dangers."

Roco shot back, "We want you to return us to Orego! Then we will spare your life."

Senor Alvarez replied, "Gentlemen, the Nekjonians have annexed your village to their new empire. Do you think they will suffer you to return home? Nay, they will kill you. I know the chieftain, and he's a ruthless son of a bitch. He leveled your village. Didn't he? If I take you to another part of Africa, you will face hostile forces. Besides, I have limited food. We will starve before we return to Orego. So I recommend we continue to Jamaica. In my world, I am an important man. I have power and powerful friends. In my civilization, you are my property. I will free you to organize your own community in Jamaica. You will have saved my life. In turn, I will show you my gratitude. If not, you kill me, and you will die in the watery wilderness of the ocean via starvation or other hostile slave ships with cannons and other weapons."

Roco called over Nimro, a priest, to consult with him. "What do you think, Nimro?" asked Roco.

Roczo interrupted, "Kill them! We should not negotiate with bloodsuckers!"

Roco stopped his brother's intervention and allowed Nimro to speak. "I share Roczo's sentiments. However, we have to compromise with the captain. Yes, he is untrustworthy, but our options are limited," said Nimro, resigned.

The captain smiled and set the course for the island in the sun—Jamaica.

At the port in Jamaica, after weeks turning into months at sea, the captain and his newly promoted first officer, Daniel Coreia, departed from the ship and headed toward the office of the port's chief administrator, Captain Jarlath Gilpatrick. He was a devout racist and a notorious drunk. He had received his commission as chief administrator of the port because he had been a spy employed by the English. He had spied on Irish rebels for the British Intelligence Service. Soon, he was discovered as a traitor by his Irish countrymen. For his protection, the British Intelligence Service relocated him to Jamaica under his new assumed name.

Captain Jarlath Gilpatrick greeted, "Benny boy, how was your expedition?" Captain Gilpatrick and Captain Alvarez were old friends. Captain Alvarez was a freelancer who was allowed via special privilege to trade within the profitable and coveted Transatlantic Triangle and the Middle Passage although he was not a British national. Captain Alvarez enjoyed these privileges for several reasons. First, he was an experienced and successful slave merchant who plied his trade on the Brazilian, Spanish, Portuguese, French, and Dutch routes. Second, he was multilingual and skilled in the acquirement of languages and dialects. Third, he was an expert double agent who was able to trade secrets among the European powers. Fourth, he was a clever spy who was able to avoid getting caught in this treacherous, dangerous, and profitable game. Finally, he was related by blood and marriage to the influential Jewish Portuguese community (mainly those in Clarendon, Jamaica).

Captain Alvarez answered, "Cap, my boy, I am saddened to report that I have a slave mutiny onboard."

Captain Gilpatrick was startled. "Right now, the niggers are in control of the ship in the dock?"

"Yes!" chimed in First Officer Daniel Coreia.

They reported the full story of the mutiny to Captain Gilpatrick.

Patiently, we waited below the deck for the double-crossing captain to return. To our dismay, a column of Redcoats surrounded and boarded the ship. They pulled three of the mutiny's leaders out and viciously whipped the rest, including me. On the wharf, they made a makeshift gallows and placed Nimro, Roco, and his brother on it. Captain Gilpatrick recited a long list of charges and asked if the leaders had a final statement—a translator was provided—before going to "a slave plantation in Hell."

Nimro predicted, "Jamaica will produce many black sons who will lead the final rebellion to the final victory."

Next, Roco said, "Ben, you are a bloodsucking flea whom I should've stepped on. I should have listened to my brother. By the will of our gods and ancestors, you and your family will pay for what you've done to my people."

Then his brother recited the universal mantra, "Better to die a free man than as a slave!"

They swung on the gallows as an example to us. Afterward, Captain Gilpatrick proclaimed, "Take these terrorists to the port in New Orleans, Louisiana. Jamaica doesn't admit terrorists through her ports." The ship set sail for New Orleans.

Source: Alabama Department of Archives and History, Montgomery, Alabama. Nathan H. Glick pen-and-ink drawings, LPR92.

3

PARADISE LOST

L IKE CATTLE DELIVERED to the marketplace, we were unloaded from the ship in New Orleans. Quickly, we were processed for sale in the marketplace. Wholesale buyers and plantation owners gathered around to gawk, inspect, and choose the slaves they wished to purchase. Using dirty hands, they inspected our dental hygiene and our whole bodies (including the pubic areas for both males and females). It was very similar to a farmer purchasing livestock. Like cattle, we were branded and separated from family and friends.

A plantation owner was closely inspecting me. He was from the Province of Georgia—a rich Southern plantation owner named Gerald Elliott. He outbid two planters from Charles Town, Carolina, and the delta region of the Mississippi River. Upon payment, he took me on a wagon to his plantation in the Province of Georgia. In Georgia, I fully realized a war was in full swing. It was 1776; the American Revolution was more than a year old. Gerald Elliott was very distracted because his eldest son was an officer under General George Washington and had joined the Georgian Militia. The youngest son, Gerald Elliott Jr., resided on the plantation. Gerald Elliott was a sadistic master to his slaves. He treated the slaves worse than his farm animals. For example, he whipped them, at times, without any just cause or logical reason.

One day, a neighbor visited my master to share news about the progress of the war and about his sons' welfare. The visitor's name was Baron Harald von

Kunhardt. He owned a plantation north of Mr. Elliott's plantation. He was a retired Prussian military officer and a mercenary who had fought in the French and Indian War (the Seven Years' War) from 1756 to 1763. Prussia had been an ally of Great Britain and the American colonies during the war against France and her allies. At the end of the war, he was granted land and a pension (with decorations and upgrades of rank) for his outstanding service during the war.

In actuality, he was a Prussian intelligence officer sent to observe Britain's emerging superpower status, especially in North America. His superior, Frederick the Great, was entertaining the possibility of grabbing colonies in North America in order to dilute his ally's emerging superpower and to energize a Prussian navy to compete with France's navy. During the Revolutionary War, the baron became a double agent under the British spymaster Dr. John Brown (based in Manhattan). He reported to the Prussians and to the British about the revolutionaries' strength in the Southern colonies and territories. Plus, he monitored the covert and overt involvement of the French, Spanish, and Dutch support for the American rebels. In addition, he recruited spies within the ranks of the military police and George Washington's bodyguards. They were German mercenaries recruited by the Americans. Baron von Kunhardt called his network of spies the Iron Cross Orchestra, in memory of the Teutonic Knights.

Baron von Kunhardt noticed me on the porch. He asked Mr. Elliott about my age and background, and Mr. Elliott told him I was seven years old and that he had recently purchased me in New Orleans. Baron von Kunhardt persuaded Mr. Elliott to agree to a profitable sale. I was sold to a new master. The sale turned out to be a blessing in disguise because Baron von Kunhardt was purchasing an adopted son instead of a domestic slave. Yep, I was going to be Moses growing up in Pharaoh's household, where I would be trained by my oppressor's standards. Thus, I would be able to lead my people to Zion—the Promised Land—back to Africa.

Baron von Kunhardt's attachment to me was due to sentimental reasons. In the French and Indian War, he was wounded during a ferocious battle (the Battle of Montreal in 1760) with French and Indian forces. Luckily, he was taken prisoner by a young French officer named Jean-Bertrand Aristide. Monsieur Aristide was of minor French nobility. He was an intelligence officer and a scientist with the French army. He was disillusioned when he learned his fellow nobleman, Commander Francois Gaston de Levis, was forced to surrender Montreal on the orders of the French governor, Marquis de Vaudreuil, due to lack of supplies and inefficient logistics. They wanted to fight and believed they would have won the battle in a similar fashion to the Battle of Sainte-Foy. However, the French governor's order prevailed over their objections. Later, Colonel Aristide became a leader in the French Revolution along with General Lafayette, a veteran of the American Revolution.

Privately, he aggressively interrogated a severely wounded and semiconscious Baron von Kunhardt about his role in the battle. Skillfully, he gleaned the information of the Prussian and British spy networks in North America. Prophetically, he postulated the political climate would change in France. He informed Commander de Levis of his decision to deceive the British and Prussian intelligence services and get them to employ him as a disgruntled French intelligence officer. He wanted his commander to persuade Paris and Louis XV to allow him to remain in Montreal. Hopefully, he would be able to gather intelligence that France could use to recoup her losses in the near future. Commander de Levis persuaded his superiors to approve Colonel Aristide's plan.

In the interim, Aristide and his Mohawk assistant (a female) nursed Baron von Kunhardt's wounds. Grateful, Baron von Kunhardt introduced Colonel Aristide to Dr. John Brown. As a matter of fact, Baron von Kunhardt married Colonel Aristide's Mohawk assistant. Unfortunately, she and their baby died during childbirth. In mourning, Dr. Brown arranged for the baron to relocate to the Province of Georgia—just in time for the American Revolution—where he would provide vital information.

Returning to the baron's interest in me, he saw me as a replacement for his stillborn son. After all, the baron was childless and swore to remain a widower after his beloved wife's death. In fact, the baron was an abolitionist—a convert to Dr. John Brown's feverish obsession with the abolition of slavery. However, he had to choose a role that would blend him into the background of the stage he was performing on—a plantation owner in the Deep South. Heck, it is written, "When in Rome, do as the Romans do." Therefore, he chose a benevolent slave owner as the perfect cover for his espionage activities in Georgia and in the South.

He noticed my former master had named me Clarence Thomas Elliott after my purchase. He asked me my African name. I told him, "Kenjo!" In turn, he named me Afrika Kenjo von Kunhardt. The choice of my name is obvious—the continent, my ancestral name, and his surname. In secret, he made me a free man and adopted me as his son. Incidentally, I found favors in his eyes. He set about to teach me everything he knew. He hired private tutors (whom he trusted) to homeschool me in a rigorous curriculum—including English, French (and other Romance languages), German, Latin, Greek, Hebrew, geography, rhetoric, the natural and social sciences, mathematics, history, philosophy, and others. He superseded the building blocks of education—reading, writing and arithmetic—when he diagnosed me as a child prodigy. He commented that my brain was like a sponge and that I was able to absorb data with an unparalleled concentration. Further, the baron explained that I had an eidetic memory (total recall), enabling me to be a polymath (e.g., Leonardo Da Vinci) and a polyhistor (e.g., Gottfried Wilhelm Leibniz—a personal friend of the baron). He noted that a genius of my caliber comes around every two hundred years, perhaps every millennium. He warned me that great power comes with great responsibility—genius is saddled with both blessings and curses. The curses consist of a lack of emotion and compassion, coldness, amorality, arrogance, a superiority complex, psychopathic behavior, and attraction to the darker forces of nature—especially if the curses are triggered by a trauma (e.g., childhood trauma experienced in slavery).

On the brighter side, I memorized the Holy Bible, to his delight. A Lutheran by background, he was a strong believer in the Bible. He drilled me to read the Bible and pray—three times per day. He encouraged my belief in Jesus Christ and His purpose of dying on the cross for the Jews and the gentiles. I became a literal believer in the inerrant Word of God. He was able to answer most of my questions about life. He was the son of a theologian and a professor (a noble). The Prussian intelligence officer (who spoke German, French, and English and had a working knowledge of various Native Indian languages) was a trained engineer also.

In the outdoors, he taught me horseback riding, the use of firearms, boxing, martial arts and sciences, the art of war, various sports, wilderness survival, swimming, and other pursuits. For the finer things in life, he taught me dinner etiquette, ballroom dancing, and how to court women (after all, I was growing up into a tall, dark, and handsome young man).

During rides in the woods, he would share his vision of a united Germany. "One Germany under a Prussian emperor would be invincible," he believed. He continued, "Germany, composed of Prussia, Austria—the German part of the Austrian Empire—Bavaria, Swiss Germans, and other minor and major German states, would be the greatest empire in history. France, England, and Russia would oppose a united Germany, of course. War would be inevitable with our natural enemies—better yet, competitors. So what? We fight, conquer, and rule the world. It is our birthright. The time of the Romans has passed. On the horizon, the time of the Germans is upon us." He joked, "What do you get when three Englishmen meet?"

I replied, "What?"

He answered, "An empire! What do you get when three Frenchmen meet?"

I inquired, "What?"

He jovially responded, "Oui surrender!" He finally added, "What do you get when three Prussians meet?"

I asked, "What?"

He exclaimed, "A war!" Piercing through me with his steel-blue eyes under his furrowed, blond, and bushy brow, he lectured, "Yes, three Germans meeting will end in a world war. In other words, Prussia, Austria, and Bavaria—and other satellite German states—uniting into a super German state would be a threat to England, France, and Russia. However, we would be able to aptly defend ourselves. We don't need to look further than the Seven Years' War— Frederick the Great, with the help of Providence, was able to defend Prussia against Sweden, France, Austria, and Russia. We stood alone. Britain provided funds but a very small expeditionary force. Our success is a testament to the Teutonic character and the German spirit. Definitely, Germany must unite into an empire of the ages. If the world should rise against us, then we fight to final victory—make the whole world a German colony. This is my dream—a

German empire and world domination!" (He authored a book that was published in Prussia about the idea of a united Germany).

Returning to reality, the Revolutionary war continued to rage in the thirteen colonies. Gerald Elliott Sr. received a letter from his eldest son, an intelligence officer working under General George Washington at the front. He confided that General Washington, Major General Alexander Hamilton, Major General Nathanael Greene, Ambassador Benjamin Franklin, and Baron Friedrich Wilhelm Augustus von Steuben (a Prussian serving as a general in the Continental Army) believed Baron Harald von Kunhardt was a spy working for the Redcoats. They had mounted an investigation in the hope of gathering evidence against him. He wanted his father to keep an eye on the plantation and its master. In case of any unusual activities, he told his father to report to him. Thus, Mr. Elliott and his family began to observe the plantation and to bribe white employees to divulge happenings. Baron von Kunhardt, with Teutonic thoroughness, maintained his clandestine correspondence with Dr. Brown and the education of his adopted son.

During my adopted father's covert Western civilization indoctrination of me, my former master's son, Gerald Elliott Jr., noticed my evolution—a slave developing into a Southern gentleman. He was a pompous, arrogant, and sadistic individual who wantonly raped slaves on his plantation. Worse, he was murderous and incestuous—he raped and killed (by accident, to prevent her from screaming) his own sister, Libby Elliott. To cover the crime, he accused me of perpetrating the abominable transgression.

In my defense, the baron made it clear that I was in his presence when the crime occurred. Plus, he would sue and shoot anyone—a lynch mob was formed to render justice—who trespassed on his property. He recommended they file charges against me in a court of law. He was planning to send me behind the British lines in New York because he didn't trust the local courts despite my innocence.

An enraged Gerald Elliott Sr., believing his son's story, cursed the baron as a nigger lover and a traitor—a British spy. In response, my father demanded proof of his accusation on the penalty that he would sue Mr. Elliott for slander and defamation of character. In addition, he insinuated that Mr. Elliott's son might be the culprit in his daughter's demise. Explosively, Mr. Elliot Sr. challenged the baron to a duel—a duel that Baron von Kunhardt couldn't avoid. He had to honor the duel, or he would risk losing respect and reputation among his peers—as a Prussian aristocrat and military officer—the baron knew and practiced the tradition well.

Besides making preparations for the upcoming duel, the baron informed Dr. Brown (who was my adopted godfather) of the new developments. He requested escorts to transport me to New York City. He furnished me with my Certificate of Freedom and a Seaman's Protection Certificate, in case the British ship was captured by French or Spanish or Dutch naval vessels. In case of his death during the duel, he authorized the liquidation of his assets (excluding the slaves, whom he willed to be free upon his departure via death or migration) and the transfer of the monies to me in care of my godfather.

While my father was preoccupied with the preparation of his will and the duel, I started to lay the groundwork for a slave revolt—the grandest revolt in the American colonies. At thirteen, I began to live up to my child prodigy moniker. I turned within, upon my innate skills (the Kenjonian spirit) and my nurtured skills (the Western education received from the baron). In secrecy (without the knowledge of the baron and his white overseers), I expeditiously unfolded my master plan. I forged letters (using the baron's stationary and seal) to British agents (I was aware of the baron's espionage activities via my innate inquisitiveness) stationed in Georgia—to instigate slave revolts across the province. Plus, I commanded them to encourage hostile Native Indian allies to attack from Florida and from the west. I (in the name of the baron) ordered the Southern network of spies and operatives to coordinate their attacks for maximum effect. They were to be mobilized on the date of the duel. I wanted them to believe that the spymaster and the baron wanted them to distract Major General Nathanael Greene's Southern Command forces with the diverse uprisings.

Next, I sowed the seeds of rebellion among the baron's slaves. They were always supportive of me. They stood by me during the false accusation of rape and murder by the Elliott family. I used their support to spread my propaganda among them. The propaganda was made up of truths, half-truths, and lies. For example, I planted the idea that the baron's slaves would be killed (by the Elliott

plantation) if he failed to return from the duel. In a Machiavellian way, I es-
chewed any guilt derived from my deception—the end would justify the means.
I organized an elite and special force among the slaves headed by a loyal mason
nicknamed Three-Fingered Jack (he had lost two fingers in a stonecutting accident, and he was of a giant stature). We sorted out security risks (known
collaborators who were listed as spies, mostly domestic slaves) from among the
masses. We eliminated them via arranged fatal accidents. The handpicked elite
guard knew of the plan, while the masses knew that something was brewing
in the air. In the cover of darkness, I organized drills and strategy planning
(knowledge I learned from the baron) with my elite unit. I advised them to pass
the word, selectively, to other plantations.

On the night before the duel, after the baron had retired to bed, I held a
secret meeting. I began, "Gentlemen! I'm a very young lad of thirteen years.
Howbeit, it is written in the Bible, 'A little child shall lead them.' I, the adopted
son of our master, have seen to it that you are well fed and well rested in preparation for the rebellion—if our master should not return from his duel. Many of
you might wonder if our rebellion is moral or just. Aren't the white men fighting a revolution against the so-called oppression and tyranny of the Redcoats?
The hypocrites declared in their Declaration of Independence that 'all men are
created equal.' As a matter of fact, let me recite their unanimous Declaration
of Independence of the thirteen united States of America, passed in Congress
on July 4, 1776."

> When in the Course of human events, it becomes necessary for one
> people to dissolve the political bands which have connected them with
> another, and to assume among the Powers of the earth, the separate and
> equal station to which the Laws of Nature and of Nature's God entitle
> them, a decent respect to the opinions of mankind requires that they
> should declare the causes which impel them to the separation.

**We hold these truths to be self-evident, that all men are created
equal, that they are endowed by their Creator with certain unalien-
able Rights, that among these are Life, Liberty, and the pursuit of**

Happiness. That to secure these rights, Governments are instituted among Men, deriving their just powers from the consent of the governed. That whenever any Form of Government becomes destructive of these ends, it is the Right of the People to alter or to abolish it, and to institute new Government, having its foundation on such principles and organizing its powers in such form, as to them shall seem most likely to effect their Safety and Happiness. Prudence, indeed, will dictate that Governments long established should not be changed for light and transient causes; and accordingly all experience hath shown that mankind are more disposed to suffer, while evils are sufferable, than to right themselves by abolishing the forms to which they are accustomed. But when a long train of abuses and usurpations pursuing invariably the same Object evinces a design to reduce them under absolute Despotism, it is their right, it is their duty, to throw off such Government, and to provide new Guards for their future security. Such has been the patient suffrance of these Colonies; and such is now the necessity which constrains them to alter their former Systems of Government. The history of the present King of Great Britain is a history of repeated injuries and usurpations, all having in direct object the establishment of an absolute Tyranny over these States. To prove this, let Facts be submitted to a candid world.

He has refused his Assent to Laws, the most wholesome and necessary for the public good.

He has forbidden his Governors to pass laws of immediate and pressing importance, unless suspended in their operation till his Assent should be obtained; and when so suspended, has utterly neglected to attend to them.

He has refused to pass other Laws for the accommodation of large districts of people, unless those people would relinquish the right of Representation in the Legislature, a right inestimable to them and formidable to tyrants only.

He has called together legislative bodies at places unusual, uncomfortable, and distant from the depository of their Public Records, for the sole purpose of fatiguing them into compliance with his measures.

He has dissolved Representative Houses repeatedly, for opposing with manly firmness his invasions on the rights of the people.

He has refused for a long time, after such dissolutions, to cause others to be elected; whereby the Legislative Powers, incapable of Annihilation, have returned to the People at large for their exercise; the State remaining in the meantime exposed to all the dangers of invasion from without, and convulsions within.

He has endeavored to prevent the population of these States; for that purpose obstructing the Laws for Naturalization of Foreigners; refusing to pass others to encourage their migration hither, and raising the conditions of new Appropriations of Lands.

He has obstructed the Administration of Justice, by refusing his Assent to Laws for establishing Judiciary Powers.

He has made Judges dependent on his Will alone, for the tenure of their offices, and the amount and payment of their salaries.

He has erected a multitude of New Offices, and sent hither swarms of Officers to harass our people, and eat out their substance.

He has kept among us, in times of peace, Standing Armies without the Consent of our legislatures.

He has affected to render the military independent of and superior to the Civil Power.

He has combined with others to subject us to a jurisdiction foreign to our constitution, and unacknowledged by our laws; giving his Assent to their acts of pretended legislation.

For quartering large bodies of armed troops among us:

For protecting them, by a mock Trial, from Punishment for any Murders which they should commit on the Inhabitants of these States:

For cutting off our Trade with all parts of the world:

For imposing taxes on us without our Consent:

For depriving us in many cases, of the benefits of Trial by Jury:

For transporting us beyond Seas to be tried for pretended offenses:

For abolishing the free System of English Laws in a neighboring Province, establishing therein an Arbitrary government, and enlarging its Boundaries so as to render it at once an example and fit instrument for introducing the same absolute rule into these Colonies:

For taking away our Charters, abolishing our most valuable Laws, and altering fundamentally, the Forms of our Governments:

For suspending our own Legislatures, and declaring themselves invested with Power to legislate for us in all cases whatsoever:

He has abdicated Government here, by declaring us out of his Protection and waging War against us.

He has plundered our seas, ravaged our Coasts, burned our towns, and destroyed the lives of our people.

He is at this time transporting large armies of foreign mercenaries to compleat the works of death, desolation and tyranny, already begun with circumstances of Cruelty & perfidy scarcely paralleled in the most barbarous ages, and totally unworthy the Head of a civilized nation.

He has constrained our fellow Citizen taken Captive on the high Seas to bear Arms against their Country, to become the executioners of their friends and Brethren, or to fall themselves by their Hands.

"'He has excited domestic insurrections amongst us, and has endeavored to bring on the inhabitants of our frontiers, the merciless Indian Savages, whose known rule of warfare, is an undistinguished destruction of all ages, sexes and conditions.

In every stage of these Oppressions We have Petitioned for Redress in the most humble terms: Our repeated Petitions have been answered only by repeated injury. A Prince, whose character is thus marked by every act which may define a Tyrant, is unfit to be the ruler of a free people.

Nor have We been wanting in attention to our British brethren. We have warned them from time to time of attempts by their legislature to extend an unwarrantable jurisdiction over us. We have reminded them of the circumstances of our emigration and settlement here. We have appealed to their native justice and magnanimity, and we have conjured them by the ties of our common kindred to disavow these usurpations, which would inevitably interrupt our connection and correspondence.

They too have been deaf to the voice of justice and of consanguinity. We must, therefore, acquiesce in the necessity, which denounces our Separation, and hold them, as we hold the rest of mankind, Enemies in War, in Peace Friends.

We, therefore, the Representatives of the United States of America, in General Congress, assembled, appealing to the Supreme Judge of the world for the rectitude of our intentions, do, in the name, and by authority of the good People of these Colonies, solemnly publish and declare, That these United Colonies are, and of Right ought to be Free and Independent States; that they are Absolved from all Allegiance to the British Crown, and that all political connection between them and the State of Great Britain, is and ought to be totally dissolved; and that as Free and Independent States, they have full power to levy War, conclude Peace, contract Alliances, establish Commerce, and to do all other Acts and Things which Independent States may of right do. And for the support of this Declaration, with a firm reliance on the Protection of Divine Providence, we mutually pledge to each other our Lives, our Fortunes and our sacred Honor.

"The declaration was approved by the thirteen colonies: the Carolinas, Connecticut, Delaware, Georgia, Maryland, Massachusetts, New Hampshire, New Jersey, New York, Pennsylvania, Rhode Island, and Virginia. Gentlemen! If I may borrow from the Roman Brutus, 'Lend me your ears!' The signers of the declaration I recited to you are the owners of slaves. Slaves who are created equal to them as per their testimony. Don't we stand on a higher moral ground? We live among them. Let's compare their privileged lives to our wretched lives. Don't we stand on a higher moral ground? Are you listening to me? If they are living under oppression, we are living under the devils' domination—in hell. Don't we stand on a higher moral ground? The content of the declaration befits our miserable lives and treatment by the colonials better than our masters' comfortable lives and treatment by the Redcoats. Don't we stand on a higher moral ground? Therefore, if our masters reserve the inalienable right to declare a revolution on the Redcoats, then we, in turn, reserve the inalienable right to declare a revolution on our masters. Don't we stand on a higher moral ground? Gentlemen, let's eschew any guilt and hesitation you may feel about our actions because we stand on a higher moral ground.

"Gentlemen, we must wage a total war. We are going to raze the plantations like King Saul's destruction of Edom or Joshua's destruction of Jericho or Imperial Rome's destruction of Carthage. We must wage a total war—a war that will destroy our masters' families and property. You might wonder if we are too overzealous in our objectives. Shouldn't family and property be untouchable and sacred? Don't allow yourselves to forget that we are property—their slaves. Don't allow yourselves to forget that they raped, pillaged, separated, and murdered our women and children. In war, everything is equal. In war, we kill or we will be killed. In war, we should not hold anything sacred. In the Machiavellian art of war, crimes are committed by losers. In our war, we fight for freedom or death. We fight to win or to the death. In war, the colors are black and white—no gray area, no middle ground.

"Yes, most of us will die during our revolution. Naturally, many of you are afraid of death. Gentlemen, we must overcome the fear of her sting because we will meet death one day. At least let us meet death on our own terms. Let us greet death as free men rather than shackled children. Let us salute death in all our glory rather than salute her in self-pity. Let us hail death after living for one day as a lion rather than living for one hundred years as a donkey, a beast of burden. If I may borrow a quote from Julius Caesar, let's welcome death once rather than a thousand times via cowardice. Don't let death define us. We must define death. We must dictate how we die.

"That's right, gentlemen! Our freedom will not be given to us on a silver platter. We must earn our freedom. We must fight for our freedom. We must die for our freedom. Only war and death will liberate us from slavery. In other words, only Mars and Pluto will set us free. We must fight! It is better to earn a prize than to receive a gift. A prize won by our blood, sweat and, tears is more cherished than a gift handed to us. We must fight! Let's not depend on the white man's welfare; instead, let's depend on the black man's warfare. We must fight! In response to the white man's constitution—it was written after the Revolution, but I suspected the United States would form a constitutional government—and declaration, we must demand restitution and reparation from our oppressors. We must fight! We have to crush grapes to make wine. We must fight! Women and men must fight side by side. We must fight!

"Why do we fight? We fight for ourselves. We fight for our women. We fight for our children. We fight for our children's children. We fight for the content depicted in their declaration. Most of all, we fight for the freedom of our mother—Mother Africa. Alas, our mother's crown is thrown upon a heap of dung. Let's take up the crown with a sword. Let's sanitize the crown—with a revolution—and return it to the head of Mother Africa. Let's make Mother Africa proud. Let's make a smiling Mother Africa the mistress of the world again."

A thunderous applause and ovation greeted the end of my preaching. In unison, they shouted, "Hail Afrika! Hail Afrika! Hail Afrika! Freedom or death! Freedom or death! Freedom or death!"

Then I knew I had gotten my war—the beginning of a revolution to unite Africa, supplanting the Kenjonian Empire, because I had begun to think as an African instead of a Kenjonian via my interaction with the other African and Creole slaves. Once more, I was thirteen years of age.

In the misty morning, the undercover agents took me to the coastline to board a ship going to New York. I bade farewell to Three-Fingered Jack and to my father for the last time. I slipped a poem that I had composed into the baron's hand. It was a farewell poem and a poem forecasting the storm that was going to tear through Georgia—the brewing of the perfect storm on the horizon, a storm I had brewed in a caldron and flavored with spices such as salt and black and red peppers. A caldron whose cover was to be blown off by a violent volcanic eruption, spurting a cloud of aroma over Georgia and delighting the nostrils and taste buds of War and his two aides de camp—Fear and Terror. The three warriors would hungrily race to the scene of the banquet, where they would join the Four Horsemen of the Apocalypse at the dining table. The baron read the poem:

Heaven's Tears

By Afrika Kenjo von Kunhardt

The sky is gray, grave, and growling
There is no moon, yet the wolves are howling.
Up yonder, lightning strikes, and the thunder keeps rolling
As impregnated clouds morbidly march as if they're in mourning.

I think to myself, a storm looms
On the horizon, where echoes of the riotous weather produce a boom.
Immediately, I withdraw into a corner of my room
Comfort by ominous gloom and pending doom.

Don't worry my dear; instead, be of good cheer
There's nothing for you to fear,
The falling of the raindrops you hear
Are just Heaven's tears.

After he read the poem, he wiped a tear from his eye as he folded the poem and placed it in a shirt pocket over his heart.

In an open field, the baron and Mr. Elliott went through the duel etiquette. They paced forward, turned, and shot at each other. Unluckily, the baron's pistol jammed (although it had been in proper working condition when he examined it). In turn, Mr. Elliott's bullet found its mark—in the heart of my dearly departed adopted father. He fell back and gasped in German, "Mein Preußen, lebe lang und glücklich unter einem Kaiser, einem Deutschland und einem Europa! Mein Sohn—Afrika—lebe lang und glücklich! Lang lebe Deutschland!" Then he gave up the ghost. According to his will, Dr. Brown arranged for his body to return to Prussia for a military burial.

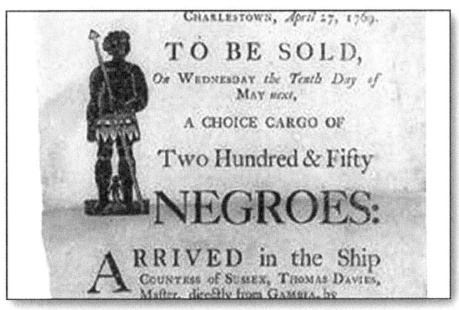

Focus on the slave trade: Millions were forcibly deported
from Africa (Image: American Antiquarian Society)

Source: http://news.bbc.co.uk/1/hi/world/africa/1523100.stm#text

Part Two

On the Run

*I know no national boundary where the Negro is concerned. The whole
world is my province until Africa is free.*

— Marcus Mosiah Garvey

4

FREE AT LAST

I SAW MANY British naval and merchant ships along the coastline. Nonetheless, my emancipating trip to New York City was uneventful. On the other hand, the lid was blown off the pot as the boiling water ran over the edges in Georgia. Following the death of the baron, the secret agents and Three-Fingered Jack ignited the powder keg of the revolts. Three-Fingered Jack and his forces leaped into action by instigating and marching to the Elliott plantation on a murderous rampage. They burned, killed, ravished, and plundered everything in their path. They were like a swarm of African locusts devouring a field. They decimated everyone and everything in sight like a swarm of Japanese hornets annihilating a European honey beehive.

Native Indian forces attacked the Georgians from the southern and western fronts. The Chickamauga, led by the legendary Dragging Canoe, terrorized the southwest of Georgia while hostile Creeks attacked southern Georgia from northern Florida (a Spanish colony). Plus, there were defections from an all-black Haitian unit commanded (with other French forces) by Marquis de Lafayette. The Haitian defectors joined the slave revolts in northeast Georgia. In addition, Redcoat regiments from the occupied cities of Savannah and Augusta, Georgia, marched against Continental Army forces sent to repress the slave rebellions and Native Indian attacks. Adding fuel to the fire, Lord Dunmore (the royal governor of Virginia, who issued an emancipation proclamation in November

1775 promising freedom to runaway slaves who fought for the British) and Sir Henry (who issued a similar edict in New York in 1779) mobilized all-black units, via ships, to Georgia to instigate and fight with the revolting slaves when news of the slave rebellion reached the northern provinces. I had created a perfect storm. A storm that would've made the baron proud based on its efficiency and effectiveness, and a storm riding the winds of war for maximum effect. I was ecstatic!

In reaction, General George Washington ordered Major General Nathanael Greene (of the Southern Command) to repress the revolts. Colonel Richard (Dick) Elliott (the eldest son of Gerald Elliott Sr.) volunteered to lead forces to quell the uprisings. Major General Greene approved his request. In turn, he quickly linked up with the unit of his brother, Captain George Elliott of the Georgian Militia. They were returning home to rescue their father and his plantation—the heart of the mini revolution.

The tide of my counterrevolution began to recede due to many reasons. Firstly, the rears of the Chickamauga (led by the illustrious Dragging Canoe) and the Creeks were threatened by Spanish and French forces. Spain, an ally of France, did not overtly support the Continental Army because she did not want to inspire revolutions in her colonies. However, she did not want a successful slave revolt and Native Indian uprisings to create a domino effect in her empire. Thus, she chose the greater of two evils (in her mind): to repress the slave rebellions and to derail the Native Indian warpath. In response to the Spanish and French mobilization, the Native Indian forces retreated to avoid being outflanked by them or to be forced into a pincer by the Continental Army and her allies.

Secondly, the French navy (with Spanish and Dutch support) stepped up her attacks on the British shipping lanes. The stalemate naval battles impeded the marine transportation of reinforcements and logistics to Georgia. Thirdly, the Redcoats had to detour, and they broke away from engagements with the Continental Army to preclude the advancement of a greater threat: regular French troops. The French troops allowed the Redcoats to chase them out of the province into a trap—a strategic ambush set up by Continental Army troops. Fourthly, the Loyalists (colonists who opposed the American Revolution) were alarmed by the slave revolts and the Native Indians raids. Many were slave own-ers who supported the Continental Army's effort to crush the rebellions. As a consequence, the Redcoats lost the goodwill and support of their colonial base (Loyalists) in the region.

Finally, the slave revolts were suppressed. Many slaves (men, women, and children) were killed in action. In the aftermath, many participants and innocent survivors were tortured and killed. After the rebellion, fifteen thousand slaves were executed in one day. Gerald Elliott Sr. escaped while his wife and young-est son were killed. Later, he reunited with his surviving sons. The sons were bent on revenge. They oversaw summary executions of the rebellion survivors. One of the survivors was Three-Fingered Jack. He was personally tortured and interrogated by Colonel Dick Elliott, Dick's father and brother, and he revealed my complicity in the rebellions. Afterward, bloody and broken, he was dragged to the gallows. He was told by the hangman to make his final statement. With a Creole accent, he stammered, "Now I'm going to die a free man. If I am guilty of fighting for the freedom of my people, then George Washington is twice as guilty for currently fighting for the so-called freedom of his people. If I'm going to be hanged for seeking my people's freedom, then George Washington should be quartered for seeking his people's so-called freedom. I am standing on the moral high ground. You would want us to believe your beloved leader is a man of freedom. To the contrary, we believe that he is a man of terror. I'm only guilty of losing the rebellion. The white man lives by the rules 'Might makes right' and 'Winner takes all.' If I'm wrong for loving my people, then I don't want to be right. African and Creole slaves, get up and stand up for your rights! African and Creole slaves, don't give up the fight! Rise up, rise up and realize you're a mighty race! Yes, they killed our prophets and heroes, but in the end, we will prevail as their conquerors. African and Creole slaves, get up and stand up for your rights! African and Creole slaves, don't give up the fight! Rise up, rise up and realize you're a mighty race. Long live Mother Africa!"

Abruptly, Colonel Dick Elliott interrupted. "Silence the nigger! Why are we allowing the terrorist monkey to profane the name of our great leader, General George Washington?" Then he commanded the hangman, "Pull the lever! It's an order!"

Others in the audience shouted, "Hang the gorilla! Hang the nigger, already!"

Three-Fingered Jack fell through the trapdoor and struggled to stay alive. The audience cursed, stoned, whipped, and spat upon his body as it swung from the end of the rope.

Three days later, Colonel Dick Elliott eulogized his late mother, Virginia Elliott, at her funeral. He started slowly. "Let us not forget the name Afrika Kenjo von Kunhardt—a name of a slave that will live in infamy. An ungrateful and wretched slave bought by my loving father. A slave sold to a traitor and a nigger lover, Baron Harald von Kunhardt—a traitor who was killed by my patriotic father." He started to raise his tone to a screaming pitch. "A demonic slave who killed my sister, mother, brother, and family and friends." He plateaued in an orgasmic and a gesticulatory fervor. "As you as my witness, I swear on my mother's grave—so help me God! I will hunt Afrika to the ends of the earth. He is a clever fox. He can run, but he cannot hide. I will flush him out of the bushes like a hunted fox. Better yet, I'll hunt him like a bloody animal. I cannot bring my mother back to life! I cannot bring my brother back to life! I cannot bring my sister back to life! I cannot bring my family and friends back to life! Howbeit, I will bring Afrika back…for justice—dead or alive! Never again should we trust a slave! Never again should we trust a nigger!"

The audience gave him a standing ovation while shouting, in unison, "Never again! Never again! Never again!" Gerald Elliott Sr. joined the chorus as he stood in his sweat-streaked brown shirt under the Georgian sun and wiped the sweat off his neatly trimmed black mustache with his white handkerchief.

The aftermath ushered in stern restrictions on slaves while steps were taken to relocate both hostile and friendly Native Indian tribes. Eventually, the latter were relocated while their lands were stolen by the white settlers.

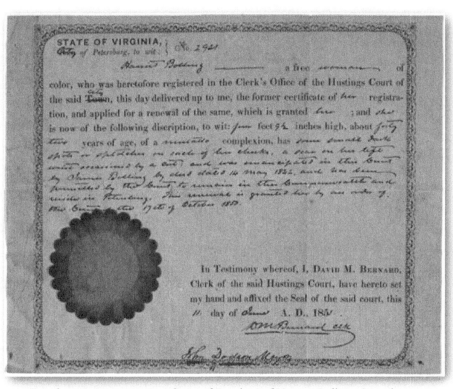

Freedom Document: Certificate of Freedom of Harriet Bolling, Petersburg, Virginia, 1851. Carter G. Woodson Collection, <u>Manuscript Division</u>. (2-2)

Source: http://rs6.loc.gov/ammem/aaohtml/exhibit/aopart2.html

5

A Teenage Runaway in New York City

D R. JOHN BROWN greeted me at the port. Finally, I was able to meet Dr. Brown for the first time. He was the son of a theologian and professor at Oxford University. He had considered following his father's footsteps into theology, but then he decided to choose the career paths of law and economics. (Later, Dr. Brown was ordained an Anglican cleric—a prerequisite for holding a professorship at Oxford). Dr. Brown was recruited into the British Intelligence Service as a student at Oxford. Most of all, he was admired for his passion. He symbolized the English tradition: for God, for king, and for country. He was born to be a knight and commander in the British Empire. Dr. Brown was a Freemason (a thirty-third-degree grand inspector general of Scottish Rite Freemasonry) and an abolitionist. He was not an abolitionist who believed that Negroes were equal to Caucasians. He thought Negroes could play a key role to enhance Britain's position as the sole superpower—where the sun never set on its empire. For example, Britain could capture Cuba (Spain), Hispaniola (France), Brazil (Portugal), and other foreign colonies if they could attract Negroes (and the indigenous people) to their side with the promise of freedom. The Negroes would be the fifth column within their enemies' territories. They could be the wasp larvae planted into the caterpillar. Thus, they could easily divide and conquer the targeted colonies while winning over the masses, including the native inhabitants of the countries. In turn, the British Empire would be like a big brother, protecting the weaker nations against malevolent bullies (other European nations). Britain would be the ruler of a world where English would supplant Latin and French as the lingua franca. Zealously, he fought to achieve his objectives by any Machiavellian means necessary.

Economically, Dr. John Brown thought planters in Cuba, Hispaniola, Brazil, and other markets were proven to be more competitive with the British markets via cheaper prices, market saturation of certain products, and other factors. He believed the abolition of slavery would level the playing field in favor of the British planters and interests. As a result, he proposed three steps to wean the British Empire off slavery: to illegalize (and enforce it with their superior navy) the international slave trade; to abolish slavery; and to seamlessly integrate the rest of the world under a benevolent British domination (the new Rome).

During the French and Indian War, he coordinated spy networks in North America and the Caribbean to expand British colonial interests at the expense of France and her allies. Currently, he was trying to prevent colonial rebels from reversing their gains and setting a precedent for other colonies to emulate. Dr. John Brown, my godfather, continued my Western civilization education.

"Master Afrika Kenjo von Kunhardt, welcome to New York! You are free at last! I was informed about your adventure in Georgia. Young man, you have lots of potential. I'm happy that you're an ally of King George instead of George Washington. Speaking of George Washington, I hope to see his treacherous corpse swinging from the end of a rope," remarked Dr. Brown.

"Nice to meet you, Godfather! Speaking of Georges, I thought any individual named George would not be hung from a tree, as per British folklore. Plus, wouldn't killing George Washington make him a martyr?" I asked.

"In regard to the folklore, Mr. Washington's neck will dispel the old wives' tale, my dear lad. He is a war criminal and a terrorist. Justice will be meted out to those committing crimes against the empire. Definitely, anyone who stands in the way of the British Empire will be crushed by the enforcement arm of its might. As for martyrdom, the Romans made a mistake with Hannibal Barca after he was defeated at Zama in Africa in 202 BC in Spain by allowing him to retire to Carthage. Later, the Romans hunted him after the realization that a dead Hannibal would be better than a live Hannibal in respect to the imperial security of Rome," lectured Dr. Brown.

On our way to my new home, he instructed me that I would be safe from bounty hunters sent from Georgia to abduct me. Plus, he didn't see any need to change my name for protection. We were behind the British lines. Plus, I would be guarded at all times.

I looked out through the window of my carriage. I inquired about New York City and the Negroes I passed. He informed me that New York City rivaled Charles Town, Carolina, in the number of slaves within its borders. He noted that some of the Negroes I saw were Black Loyalists (they were the fiercest Loyalists) who had agreed (by a contract) to fight for Britain in exchange for their freedom and compensation. Other Negroes were kept as slaves by White Loyalists, but he promised to abolish slavery as soon as London stopped fearing alienating Loyalist slave owners in NYC.

At home, he introduced me to the family physician and my new tutor— Dr. Israel Bachman. Dr. Bachman was a Jew whose parents had migrated from Holland. Dr. Bachman's parents resided in Brooklyn, where he and his sister were raised. Recently, Dr. Bachman's father had passed away. He had relocated his mother to his residence in Manhattan. In Brooklyn, Dr. Bachman's sister (who was married to a British intelligence officer) lived with her husband and son, Michael Miller Jr.

Dr. Israel Bachman was an Orthodox Jew, although his sister was very secular. He kept kosher. Dr. Bachman shared his religion with me. Obviously, he did not win a new convert, but I admired the practicality of Judaism as it pertained to nutrition and healthy living. For example, he taught me that shellfish (thinking as a physician) are forbidden from the Jewish diet because they are bottom dwellers—the scavengers of the seafloor. Besides, shellfish have to be prepared a certain way to prevent food poisoning. He gave similar reasons for pork and other "unclean" food (including the separation of dairy and meat consumption). In time, I began to limitedly espouse the Jewish dietary laws (for their practicality and not for their sacredness). I refrained from using tobacco and alcohol (except for medicinal purposes). I considered adopting a vegetarian lifestyle, but

I was incurably addicted to fish. In addition, he extolled the virtues of circumcision as it pertained to genital hygiene. In agreement, I allowed him to give me a circumcision. He told me of his family tree. Originally, Dr. Bachman's family had migrated to Holland (when it was a part of the Spanish Empire) from Spain to gain religious freedom in the Netherlands. They adopted Dutch names. Consequently, the Bachmans' descendants continued in New York.

Dr. Brown spent as much quality time with me as his work allowed. He shared philosophical insights with me as they pertained to the four spheres of influence: power, money, sex, and compassion. He believed that power and dominion would be given unto those who were able to effectively wield any of the four spheres. (As a Freemason, he loosely borrowed from the ancient Egyptian proverb that stated, "Power and dominion will be given to those who understand the power of the number thirteen.") He told me the difference between arguments and negotiations. He taught me the art of arguing and debating on various subjects. He passed on gems he had learned from his Oxford-trained theologian father, such as, "The beginning of wisdom is the fear of God" (borrowed from King Solomon) and "After wisdom comes knowledge, and after knowledge comes materialism." In other words, the hierarchy of man is composed of the spirit, the mind, and the body. Thus, we must please the spirit, the mind, and the body, in that order. Furthermore, he believed there are five spiritual, five mental, and five physical senses (sight, scent, hearing, taste, and touch)—accounting for the paranormal acquirement of intelligence (e.g., prophetic visions, etc.) recorded throughout history.

He allowed me to join his circle of friends. Many individuals would stop by his townhouse. Loyalists and Patriots would be in his company in the privacy of his home. The diverse group had a singular thread that bound them: abolition of slavery. Slave owners, slave traders, slave merchants, Jews, Quakers, Methodists, other Christians, and foreigners were members of the informal Society of Abolitionists (the Manhattan Circle). Ironically, each of the aforementioned groups directly and indirectly profited from the slave economy. However, a minority in each group tried to reform or to stop the holocaust they were perpetrating against my race. They debated about the need to free baptized Christian slaves; the inalienable rights (freedom) of slaves versus the inalienable rights (property and compensation) of slave owners; the immediate freedom of slaves vs. the graduated freedom of slaves; Britain's offer of freedom (which was honored) to Black Loyalists versus America's offer of freedom (which was not honored, like treaties with the Native Indians) to Black Patriots, and other hot subjects.

The foremost debater at my godfather's sessions was John Jay (a Dutch colonial and a Patriot), who was a rich slave owner. However, he was instrumental in reforming slavery via his later roles as the president of the influential Manumission Society and as a governor of New York. On other occasions, Colonel Tye and General Henry Clinton would visit our home to discuss assassinations (fatal and character) of leading Patriots such as General George Washington and General Benedict Arnold (before he switched sides) with the British super spy. Colonel Tye had once been a runaway slave named Titus. In 1779, he led a Loyalist brigade of Black Pioneers to attack Shrewsbury, New Jersey. The same year, British general Henry Clinton offered freedom to all slaves who joined the British ranks.

Under increased pressure from King George, Dr. Brown was able to garner evidence that Major General Alexander Hamilton, via his partly black mother, was a quadroon or an octoroon. He was unable to garner similar evidence on the Patriots' brain—Thomas Jefferson—although he believed the rumors were true. Albeit, he concealed his findings from London when he learned that Major General Alexander Hamilton was a closeted abolitionist (later, he became a member of the Manumission Society) due to Dr. Brown'sMachiavellian reasons. Therefore, he hoped, at worst, to blackmail the major general or, at best, to manipulate him via an unwitting John Jay (a friend of Major General Hamilton). In the end, he ruled out assassinations because he did not want to witness "the chickens coming home to roost." In other words, British generals could be assassinated in retaliation to the precedent he would have started.

Instead, he sowed discord within the ranks of the Continental Army and the Continental Congress. He learned through his network of Freemasons of Ambassador Benjamin Franklin's penchant for dark and deviant occult practices. He was able to collect evidence that pertained to the dark side of the ambassador. Howbeit, he was precluded from using the information in his propaganda because it was discovered that several royal family members and other powerful Britons belonged to a sister branch of Ambassador Franklin's secret society. Plus, King George and his advisors didn't want to hurt the ambassador's illegitimate son—William Franklin, the royal governor of New Jersey, a Loyalist imprisoned by the Patriots.

In the summer of 1782, it became apparent that Britain was losing the war. Loyalists, Black Loyalists, and British subjects were preparing to flee Manhattan because "the barbarians are at the gate." My godfather arranged for me to join an operative—French intelligence officer Aristide—in Montreal. He burned private and official papers in the fireplace and shipped other documents to Britain and Canada. He petitioned King George to relocate him to Montreal or Nova Scotia, where he could plan the recapture of the American colonies. Six months later, he was recalled to Britain, where he was assigned a teaching position at Oxford University. At the request of his internal and powerful enemies in the British Intelligence Service, he was secretly suspended from his commission because he had failed to obey royal orders to assassinate General George Washington in Brooklyn, New York, and in New Jersey. Lord Mansfield, a mentor, intervened on his behalf to advocate my godfather's position with King George. Lord Mansfield, in the Somerset case, outlawed slavery in England in 1772. The Somerset case involved three runaway Jamaican slaves who had escaped to England.

Dr. Bachman opted to stay in New York to take care of his infirm mother and to open a school for Jewish boys in NYC. Secretly, he was retained on the British payroll, and he developed a political relationship with the Patriot John Jay and, later, Major General Alexander Hamilton. Dr. Bachman's sister and her family migrated to London. Dr. Israel Bachman saw me off to Montreal. He wept when I boarded the ship and bid my farewell.

**Runaway advertisement taken from a New York
newspaper in British Colonial New York**

**(Albeit, slavery's stronghold became freedom's refuge during the
American Revolution—courtesy of the Redcoats for political reasons)**

*"Indeed, New York City had more slaves than any other North America
city during parts of the 17th and 18th centuries. And New York State
was one of the last in the North to abolish slavery. Meanwhile, slaves
built Wall Street's wall, the first city hospital, the first city hall, roads
and churches. Some 20,000 slaves are believed buried under six acres
of Lower Manhattan in what was known among a few historians as
the African Burial Ground."*

— KEN OLSEN FOR TOLERANCE.ORG, 2005

**Source: Slavery in New York. A Landmark Exhibition by the New
York Historical Society (http://www.nyhistory.org or http://www.
slaveryinnewyork.org)**

6

ESCAPE TO NORTH OF THE BORDER AND BEYOND THE POND

I N MONTREAL, I continued my education under Colonel Aristide's supervision. I learned about the Mohawks' culture and the history of Montreal. The history included a black slave named Marie-Joseph Angélique, who was hanged for burning the house of her owner in 1734. She set it ablaze when she learned that she had been sold to another owner. Other slaves met similar fates for lesser offenses, including a slave who was broken on the wheel, a grisly process in which the condemned person's limbs were smashed with iron bars and the mutilated corpse raised up for public display on a cartwheel. Even more atrocious punishments were meted out to other rebellious slaves.

After two years, Colonel Aristide reluctantly returned to Paris one year after the Paris Peace Treaty of 1783. Apparently, Paris had realized the American Revolution had consolidated her power over the former colonies. In addition, France was enjoying a good relationship with the new republic. Moreover, Dr. Brown's successor in North America was not as pliable as the good doctor, from Paris's perspective. Therefore, we set sail for France in 1784.

In Paris, Duke Francois Gaston de Levis awarded a teaching position to Colonel Aristide at the prestigious Ecole Militaire (in actuality, it was a military academy reserved for the sons of poor gentry, including poor minor nobility).

The Ecole Militaire graduated illustrious alumni, including Emperor Napoleon Bonaparte (developing a young master conductor of the French artillery orchestra); Haitian mulatto Commander Alexander Sabes Petion, and me. As a matter of fact, Napoleon graduated when I was accepted to the institution on a commendation from Colonel Aristide's mentor, Duke Francois Gaston de Levis. The school accepted me on the grounds that I had been adopted by the late Baron Harald von Kunhardt, a Prussian aristocrat. Personally, I was a descendant of Kenjonian nobility, with direct lineage from the Imperial Dynasty of the Kenjonian Empire.

My school days proved to be the best time of my life. My military education was indispensable to my military career. My roommate, Jean-Louis Belmont, was a source of knowledge and inspiration. Jean-Louis was the son of a French nobleman and a *boyarishna* (a Russian noblewoman). He was the most popular cadet at the school—a talented rider, fencer, and marksman. Monsieur Belmont was a handsome young man with a perfect symmetry. Hence, he was able to parlay his charisma and good looks to attract the most beautiful women—an equal-opportunity lover who dated French, Russian, African, Jewish, Muslim, and other types of women. In turn, he had to fight a few duels with jealous husbands and lovers. He introduced me to fine wine and beautiful women. I broke (while in France) my oath to refrain from alcohol. Nonetheless, I didn't consume alcohol to the point of drunkenness. Actually, I denied myself the pleasure of strong drinks—vodka, rum, beer, and strong brandy and cognacs. On the other hand, I was very competitive with the women. Jean-Louis and I would attend ballroom dances, orgies, and other hedonistic ventures. I was caught up in my youthful indiscretions. He gave me several nicknames: the Abyssinian Prince, the Moor, the Pharaoh, the Ladies' Amour, Othello, Hannibal, Menelik, Nimrod, and others.

In cerebral activities (besides Africans' contribution to ancient Rome), he introduced me to the history of Peter the Great and Genghis Khan. Peter the Great transformed Russia from the backwater of Europe to one of the five powers of Europe. On his return from a Western European tour, he Westernized the institutions of Russia. Peter the Great introduced Western civilization to Russia. I inquired about the relationship of Russia and Africans. He responded,

"Today, slavery is alive and well in my mother's country, but our slaves—white—are our fellow countrymen. These slaves sold themselves into slavery to make ends meet. My mother's family owns many slaves. In Russia, slavery is not based on race but on class. In regard to Africans and Peter the Great, we have an interesting relationship with Africans." He fetched a book from his study, and he quoted, verbatim:

For the accomplishments of Ibrahim Petrovitch Gannibal are proof of what any man—despite his colour—could rise to, given the opportunity. Ibrahim was treated as no less than a member of the royal family at court and, in the biographical notes on him written either by his wife or by someone in her family shortly after his death, the following statement is made:

"He (Peter) wished to make examples of them and put (Russians) to shame by convincing them that out of every people and even from among wild men—such as Negores, whom our civilized nations assign exclusively to the class of slave, there can be formed men who by dint of application can obtain knowledge and learning and thus become helpful to their monarch."

To a divine rights monarch like Peter whose relationship to a nation of serfs was entirely paternalistic, a child as a personal gift or possession could only be regarded as one of his own kith and kin. Indeed, at the eight-year-old Ibrahim's baptism, the Emperor himself was his godfather, while his godmother was the Queen of Poland.

Although, as we now realize, no Blackamoor at any 18th century European court was merely decorative, in Ibrahim's case, Peter's expectations for him were as loaded with responsibility as those he would have had for his own son. If he was the Emperor whose patriotic duty it was to drag Russia spiritually and intellectually out of its Byzantine backwardness and into the future of the Enlightenment, then it would literally be Ibrahim's responsibility to care for his adopted country's physical formation and his defence of it. In 1717 the young blackamoor was sent to France for an education in both civil and military engineering. He studied at the Ecole d'Artillerie of La Fere under the brilliant Bernard Forest de Belidor and afterward, at the Ecole d'Artillerie of Metz, an institution founded by the illustrious Sebastien Le Preste, Marquis de Vauban.

Besides the education which prepared him for his long life of government service, Ibrahim returned from France with something he obviously regarded just as importantly—a name. Like any black kid today reaching back through time to clutch at whatever historical straw of affirmation he can reach for, Ibrahim not only identified as his model but appropriated as his surname that of the Carthaginian general, Hannibal. Although it could be argued that like Hannibal, he knew that he too would soon enough attain the rank of general, Ibrahim's choice probably betrayed an almost adolescent edge of race conscious defiance considering the threat this Punic potentate had once posed to Rome. Perhaps a better understanding of what Ibrahim intended to imply with his new name can be gathered from what we know today regarding one of the stock theater characters of his time. Sofonbisba, a relative of the historical Hannibal, was easily the most popular of the 18th century heroines. During that period alone more than forty works, either operas or dramas, were composed with hers as the central story. It would appear that the proud African queen who fought Roman occupation to the point of committing suicide had become the personification of independence for a number of European states that were growing increasingly irritated with Hapsburg hegemony.

He closed the book and returned it to his study. Then he fetched other Russian books with French translations. He began to teach me about Genghis Khan. "Genghis Khan built the first modern army in the world. He promoted officers based on merit instead of on nobility. Like Peter the Great, he invited Chinese engineers and scientists—in Russia's case, Western Europeans—to enhance his country's technology, urban infrastructure, and rural agriculture. Like Peter the Great in the use of Western educators, he used Chinese educators to improve the educational system of the masses. Genghis Khan developed the postal system, commerce, military, and organization that influence Russia—although we downplay it—even today. The empire of Genghis Khan was four times the size of the empire of Alexander the Great and twice the size of the Roman Empire. It is noteworthy; Europe would've been a different environment if a Mongol invading force on its way to Vienna and Western Europe had not been called back to the East because of the death of a Khan. After all, Genghis Khan was the most successful military commander in world history."

I was impressed with what I had learned about Peter the Great and Genghis Khan. I was inspired to mold Africans into new Africans, to pursue an agenda of a Greater Africa—a proud Mother Africa. Eureka! I had discovered my ambition! Eureka! I had discovered my destiny—it was wedded to the fate of Africa! There was a purpose to my life—a leader of a mighty race—a western civilization of Africa.

In 1788, we graduated from Ecole Militaire. King Louis XVI attended our graduation ceremony. I graduated at the top of my class. King Louis promoted Colonel Aristide to General Aristide. The late Duke Francois Gaston de Levis, who had died a year earlier, had recommended Colonel Aristide for a promotion and a transfer back to Military Intelligence. I was made second lieutenant of the artillery. However, General Aristide exempted me from the two-year mandatory military service. As an alternative, he sent me to Britain to work as a double agent. I would spy on behalf of Paris on London. Unwittingly, my godfather quickly enrolled me into Oxford University to study law and economics. Fondly, I looked back at my school days in Paris. I left before the Storm—the Storm that ravaged Paris and France. My friend and former roommate, Captain Jean-Louis Belmont, was guillotined in 1793 on the same day as his king—Louis XVI. When I learned of his death, I wept without shedding a tear. Later, I would visit his grave during my negotiations for the release of Toussaint L'Ouverture—the Haitian Revolutionary Leader.

During the American Revolution, many slaves in America fought for the British in exchange for freedom. After the war, many Black Loyalists escaped to Canada, where they formed a regiment to defend British North America, despite hostility from white colonists. In Canada, slavery was made illegal following the end of the American Revolution.

Source: (http://www.caribbeantales.org/ct_newsletter/archives/cultural_events/1/black_history_all_year_round)

7

ACROSS THE CHANNEL

A CROSS THE ENGLISH Channel, I visited England for the first time. Dr. Brown met me at the port. After a quick tour of London, we sped off to Oxford University. At Oxford, I was introduced to my roommate, Michael Miller Jr. Mr. Miller was the nephew of my former mentor, Dr. Israel Bachman. Like General Aristide, Mr. Miller was an atheist. He believed that religion was a tool used by the ruling class to blind and fetter the masses. As in the US constitution, he believed that all men were equal. He believed Negroes (because of racial discrimination and slavery), Jews (because of religious discrimination and anti-Semitism) and other minorities could only be empowered in a utopian world. A utopian world that would replace the current governments—a one-world government based on the true equality of men and bans religions and material inequality. He was writing his master's thesis on his vision for a new world.

I believed he was ahead of his time. I liked his philosophy, except I was an unwavering believer in God and his only begotten Son—Jesus Christ. If he were to wed the belief in God to his ideology, then I would be able to accept his brilliant viewpoint on the utopian politics tailored for the urban (the hammer) and rural (the sickle) masses (symbolized in an interesting logo he created for his ideology). He preached that the blood of the masses would be needed to lubricate and fuel the wheels (he borrowed symbols from the Industrial Revolution) of the people's revolution. Thereafter, he envisioned Jews (he was Jewish via his mother's lineage), Negroes (free of slavery), serfs, peasants, the urban working classes, and the rest of the world living in a "Community of Equality" governed by the religious trinity of science, technology, and reason.

Unlike my carnival time in Paris, Oxford was staid and sober. Michael Miller Jr. wasn't Jean-Louis Belmont. I returned to my alcohol-free diet and continued in the role of an apt pupil. Nevertheless, I continued to suffer from my addiction to beautiful women. We met famous people (close friends of Dr. Brown) such as the engraver William Blake and his wife, William Wilberforce, Thomas Clarkson, Granville Sharpe, Captain John G. Stedman, author Olaudah Equiano, and other luminous British abolitionists.

We attended a grand ball where I met a French countess in exile (she had escaped the French Revolution). Countess Helene de Gramont invited me to dance with her. She was drawn to my exotic beauty and my natural gracefulness on the dance floor. She was enchanted by my fluent French and my training in Paris. In turn, I was infatuated with the unhappily married countess who was thirteen years my senior. She was of a fair complexion, with seductive hazel eyes, auburn hair, succulent lips, voluptuous bosom, and a petite body. Soon, we fell into a torrid love affair—ebony and ivory coming together in perfect harmony. We were in heat—burned with a fever—the jungle fever.

Throughout our relationship, she confided in me about her unhappiness. She accused her husband of neglecting her for his passion with his mistresses and his efforts to form a royalist army to reverse the advances of the French Revolution. She had been betrayed by friends in France and lost properties to the new government in France. In response, I composed a love poem dedicated to her:

Pretty Brown Eyes

By Afrika Kenjo von Kunhardt

Pretty Brown eyes!
You are facing many problems.
Pretty Brown eyes!
Don't worry, we'll solve them.

They are breaking your heart,
Giving you headaches,
Splitting your circle apart,
And giving you heartaches.

Dry your eyes
Because your tears are falling.
I hope to soothe you with poetry or lullabies
When you're crying.

Life can be very trying.
It's a hard-knock life we are living.
We are betrayed by the ones we love, by their cheating and lying
That cut through the heart like a knife and leave us dying.

But, pretty brown eyes,
I'll always be with you.
I'll never say good-bye,
Especially when you are going through the bleak, blistering blue.

Keep your head up
And never bow down.
Always keep a positive makeup
And pick yourself up whenever you hit the ground.

Whenever you are despondent, think of me holding you tight;
Think of me taking away your fright;
Think of me having your back during your fight;
And think of me penetrating your darkness with my light.

You might think of our relationship as a dream you're drifting through
As you nocturnally meditate and admire the moon.
I say this: when you wake up, you'll find me serenely, snugly sleeping beside you,
And I promise you this: I won't be leaving you anytime soon.

Sadly, the countess was guillotined in 1793. She became another victim of the French Revolution after she returned to attend to her sick mother. A copy of my poem was discovered in her bosom after they searched her headless body. Jean-Paul Marat, a radical revolutionary leader and an inspiration to the Reign of Terror, published my poem in his newspaper—*Journal de la Republique francaise*—to embarrass her exiled widower (an *émigré* and defender of the *Ancien Regime*). Safely, I was in revolutionary Haiti when the sex scandal erupted in Europe. Even so, my true love—Helene—was taken away from me, forever.

The French Revolution spurred Mr. Miller's interest, although he thought it should have gone further to empower the masses than just the middle class and nonnoble wealthy class. At the end of our two-year program, he returned to New York City to start a newspaper. He founded one of the most influential newspapers in the world. Originally, Dr. Brown and British Intelligence secretly financed his venture, with the usual expected returns on their investment.

Speaking of British Intelligence, Dr. Brown was reinstated in his role as a British intelligence officer. British Intelligence feared the growing power of General Aristide (who had switched to the side of the revolutionaries) and his French intelligence network. They did not want Dr. Brown to be compromised by the Frenchman unsuspectingly. They were worried about the expansion of the French Revolution and the reports of exiles spreading propaganda about subversive infiltrations across Europe. So they sent Dr. Brown and me back to the New World—far away from General Aristide. They saw the opportunity to capture French colonies and recapture the American colonies (who were weak and lacked French protection) if there was a total collapse of France. Therefore, they decided to send a North American and Caribbean expert—Dr. John Brown—to the island of Jamaica. An island set in a strategic geographical location—a base from which to launch their regime change in North America and the Caribbean. Personally, King George promoted me to Lieutenant Afrika Kenjo von Kunhardt before we set out to the island of wood and water—Jamaica.

A Negro Hung Alive by the Ribs to a Gallows. Engraving by William
Blake. The Library of Congress Rosenwald Collection.

Source: http://www.wwnorton.com/nto/18century/welcome.htm

PART THREE

MARCHING FOR LIBERTY

Up, you mighty race, accomplish what you will.

— MARCUS MOSIAH GARVEY

8

WELCOME BACK TO JAMAICA

W HEN WE SAILED into the port, we saw a sign bearing the writing, "Welcome Back to Jamaica." We were met by British Intelligence, who escorted us to the headquarters and to our townhouses. The first time, I had entered Jamaica as a lowly slave. Now, I was returning as Lieutenant Afrika Kenjo von Kunhardt of His Majesty's Secret Service. I was given a tour of Jamaica. I learned the reason for its namesake—a land of wood and water. On my tour, I noticed the infrastructure, urban planning, and architecture were similar to the British designs. I observed many Irish nuns and Catholic priests attending to the schools in the colony.

In Britain, King George III had promoted Dr. John Brown to the rank of general before he sent us to Jamaica. In Jamaica, I was assigned to Dr. Brown as his adjutant. In turn, Dr. Brown provided me with a mentor to bring me up to speed with the history and the current status of Jamaica. My native mentor and briefer was Colonel Ansel Henriques. Upon our first meeting, we were drawn to each other in an uncanny manner. We were opposites, but there was an "it" factor—which was difficult to articulate—in our relationship. Promptly, we became soul mates. I could trust him with my life. In turn, he could trust me as long as there wasn't a conflict with my uncompromising vision of the future of Mother Africa.

Colonel Ansel Henriques educated me about the history of Jamaica. He started with the arrival of Christopher Columbus and his interaction with the Arawak. Then he discussed the English invasion of Jamaica in 1655. Finally, he discussed "the good, the bad, and the ugly" of the history of the Jews in Jamaica and their influence on the world at large and on the institution of slavery in particular.

Before I reiterate our dialogue, let me first describe Colonel Ansel Henriques of His Majesty's Secret Service. He was born in Saint Elizabeth, Jamaica. He was a member of the Portuguese Jewish community in Jamaica. In private (for undercover purposes), he was a merchant and an owner of a ship named *Hamita*. Colonel Henriques's father had wanted him to follow in his footsteps as a rabbi. Instead, he opted to become a merchant, and, eventually, he was recruited into the British Intelligence network. At first, he was a successful slave trader plying his trade on the lucrative routes of the Atlantic slave trade (including the profitable South American slave trade, such as the Brazilian routes and the Surinamese routes). Dr. Brown came across his dossier and recruited Colonel Henriques in the service of the British Empire. An avowed abolitionist, Dr. Brown persuaded Colonel Henriques to join his cause. Colonel Henriques resigned from the slave trade and became one of his most loyal disciples—he became the right hand man for the good doctor in Jamaica. Subsequently, we became the triple alliance representing the abolitionist wing of the British Intelligence in the Caribbean. We operated in one accord.

On a quiet evening while we were seated on the veranda of Colonel Henriques's townhouse, we enjoyed the sunset on the horizon and the dancing of the sunrays cascading the mountainside—an inspiration to a master painter. He offered me a flask of Jamaican rum. I declined and opted for a cup of unsweetened Jamaican cerasse (*Momordica charantia*) and a saucer of English biscuits.

Colonel Henriques lectured, "Originally, Jews in Portugal—and Spain— were restricted, in spite of their collective success, because of anti-Semitism. More restrictions were placed on them whenever they adapted to the new repressive systems. They were not allowed to own lands, and they were marginalized into urban professions such as commerce, medicine, and law. Ironically, soon they became very profitable professions. Without professional alternatives—via landownership and nobility—they excelled as traders, merchants, shopkeepers, middlemen, etc. Eventually, the Spanish Inquisition demanded that Muslims and Jews convert to the Catholic faith. The ones who refused were persecuted. The rest converted, but they practiced Judaism in the privacy of their homes. After Christopher Columbus's discovery of the New World, many Jews from Spain, Portugal, and Cape Verde opted to apply their innate and nurtured skills to liberate them from the yoke of the Spanish Inquisition. They hoped for religious freedom in the Americas and on the high seas. Unfortunately, the tentacles of the Spanish Inquisition reached the New World.

"In 1655, Lord Protector Oliver Cromwell sent General Robert Venables and Admiral William Penn to capture Cuba and Hispaniola from the Spaniards. Miserably, they failed and decided to invade Jamaica instead. They asked the Iberian Jews for help. In exchange, they guaranteed the Jews their religious freedom. Thus, the Portuguese Jews sabotaged the Spaniards while their slaves escaped to the mountains. The British won the Anglo-Spanish War in 1660. Cromwell beheaded Penn and Venables because they had failed to capture Hispaniola. Then Oliver Cromwell welcomed the Iberian Jews to Britain and the British Empire because of their technical skills and knowledge, and the capital—money—they contributed to the empire. The Iberian Jews, the pirates, and the buccaneers built the British Empire. We made the legendary Port Royal, Jamaica—the world's richest city, destroyed by earthquakes and floods shortly before noon on 7 June 1692—the capital of the world. We taught the British sugar technology. This multiplied the wealth of England and drove the Industrial Revolution to new heights, making Britain the world's superpower.

"Sadly, the burden of the empire was saddled on the backs of Negroes. They were the beasts of burden that carried the empire on their backs. Here again, Jewish, Christian—allegedly, Francisco Casas, the father of

Bartolomé, requested that the Spanish crown introduce Negroes as slaves into the New World to replace the Arawaks—and Muslim scholars justified African slavery via the curse of Ham. The story of the curse of Ham was seen by most Biblical scholars as an early Hebrew rationalization for Israel's conquest and enslavement of the Canaanites, who descended from Canaan—one of the sons of Ham. Therefore, the Portuguese Jews played a role in the great holocaust of the Negroes. Howbeit, Christians, Muslims, and your own Negroid race—via tribal warfare and the sale of captives into slavery—played an equal role in it with the Iberian Jews. Today, anti-Semitism prevails against the Portuguese Jews despite our contribution to the British Empire. For example, we are not allowed to be major planters or own large plantations with many slaves under British law, although Jews are permitted to own large plantations and many slaves in Brazil and Surinam. Half of the original white planters in Brazil and Surinam were Portuguese Jews. Speaking of Surinam, the genocidal atrocities against rebellious slaves were symbolized and captured in the famous engraving by William Blake, *A Negro Hung Alive by the Ribs to a Gallows.*

"Anyway, we are petitioning London to reconsider our applications to be allowed to be planters in Jamaica. Despite our best efforts and lobbying, an influential retired chief judge—the Honorable Albert Pike—is blocking our inalienable right to own large estates of slaves. There exists a minority of abolitionists in the Jewish community of Jamaica, including me. He is an anti-Freemason, an anti-Semite, and a devout racist. He supports the antiabolitionist wing, headed by General Kevin Kirk Kinsley, of the British Intelligence. He is a thorn in the side of Dr. Brown."

I exclaimed, "Interesting! You mentioned Freemasonry. What is your view on the subject?"

He answered, "Freemasonry is one of the many secret societies that is alleged to control the world. Ultimately, they have their roots in the ancient Egyptian mysteries propagated by the Chaldeans of ancient Babylon—going back to Nimrod, the builder of the Tower of Babel, and his wife, Semiramis. Of course, Nimrod, the great hunter and ruler of men before God, is the son of Cush and the grandson of Ham. Yet he is the father of the most powerful forces on earth. On the other hand, Semiramis inspired the worship of the goddesses—Ishtar, Aphrodite, Venus, and others. In addition, Freemasonry is inspired and influenced by the medieval Knights Templar—Christian warrior-priests who took part in the Crusades—and secular Jewish secret societies, respectively.

"In the esoteric world, the secret societies symbolized by skulls and bones and crooked crosses rule—and work toward creating a New World Order. In the real world, there are five major powers: Britain, the lone superpower; France, despite its current revolution; Prussia, which is allied with the Holy Roman Empire; Austria; and Russia.

"The young American republic has the potential to join the club within a hundred years, especially if it achieves its 'Manifest Destiny.' Manifest Destiny wasn't extremely popular until the turn of the century. However, Jefferson and his ilk want to expand the new republic into Canada, Northern Mexico, the Caribbean, and the West. The Jewish nation will be able to join the club too, if it achieves its Zionist goals. The Zionist goal is to free ourselves from Babylon, the World System, and return to Palestine—Israel—to reestablish our country. Human nature, regrettably, inclined us to pave our road to success and empire building with the broken bodies of our neighbors. Indeed, history has taught us that we fertilized and watered our field of dreams with the blood and the ashes of the less fortunate. We are guilty of the evil—all races of mankind have eaten the poisonous apple. We are hungered by greed, and we thirst for power, driven to eat the flesh and to drink the blood of fellow humans. We have denigrated ourselves to the level of primitive cannibals—like lost sailors devouring one another for survival."

I looked to the full moon casting her shimmering reflection on the ocean. I inquired, "Dr. Brown informed me of your conversion to abolitionism. What is your story? What was your 'Saul struck by the light on his way to Damascus' or 'the dumb ass speaking with a man's voice forbade the madness of the prophet' moment?"

He smiled. "Very shrewd question! I was sent to investigate a Maroon raid on a plantation. My force cornered three suspicious Maroons. I shot a terrorist in the back when he tried to flee. Another Maroon blew powder into my face and cursed my family with a fatal disease. In response, I shot the bastard in his head. We took the surviving Maroon to our headquarters for further torture and interrogation.

"The next morning, my wife and six kids woke up with a strange fever. Within a few hours, they became acutely ill. I took the best doctors to attend to them, without any remarkable improvement. I visited the captured Maroon in his cell. I told him about my situation and threatened him with death if he didn't produce a supernatural or natural antidote to my family's dilemma. Calmly, he told me I had killed the son and husband of a voodoo priestess of his village. The husband had bewitched my family with obeah. My only option would be to visit the voodoo priestess to lift the curse. If not, my family would die in thirteen days. In good faith, I freed the prisoner and asked a trader to make connections with the voodoo priestess on his behalf—Portuguese Jews regularly traded with Maroons because of their Iberian connections.

"They met the voodoo priestess, a sister of an exiled Maroon known as Dutty Boukman. The Jamaican-born Dutty Boukman was chief of the Voodoo Priesthood of Haiti. She was a blind woman who had lost her sight, via torture, during one of the many Maroon wars against the Redcoats. She addressed me by my first name after I apologized for the death of her family. I implored her forgiveness since I had been following orders and I was bound by my duty. She dismissed my excuses as she explained I was guided by destiny. Fate had brought me to her to receive a message from the gods and the ancestors. She gave me an herbal concoction to medicate my family and told me that I would meet the African messiah named Kenjo. I must unite you with her brother in Haiti because you will resurrect Mother Africa. Mother Africa, again, will rule the world for eternity. She wants me to teach and to guide you—in the role of a John the Baptist, a prophet in the wilderness—on your path to the final victory for her people. She warned me that the affliction will return to my family if I double-cross you. Next, she gave me two amulets that guarantee our lives into old age. I'm wearing one as we speak. She wants me to give you the other amulet."

I refused the amulet and declared, "Jesus Christ is my amulet, and you're relieved of your duty to serve me as per the curse! If you ought to serve me, please do so according to your free will."

"Lieutenant von Kunhardt, you are a man of character—who will be a great man," complimented Captain Henriques. He continued, "My family recovered from their undiagnosed illness after I spoon-fed them the concoction. Therefore, I'm a cautious believer of the powers of obeah. I trust that you will hold my secret in confidence. I do not wish to be the subject of ridicule among my peers."

We retired to our respective sleeping quarters for the rest of the evening.

The next morning, I met Dr. Brown at his office. He was perturbed by the constant interference of Chief Judge Albert Pike in his efforts to execute his agenda. He received an invitation to have dinner with the judge on his plantation. He confided, "The good judge is a thorn in my side. I need to get some dirt on him so that he will get off my back. He thinks we have a Maroon problem and a Jewish problem. I will admit there is a legitimate concern on both fronts, but his solutions are very radical. Worse yet, he is proposing final solutions that are outrageously criminal. I cannot afford to derail my objective, as it pertains to the abolition of slavery. It is needed for the bigger picture—the recapture of our American colonies, the leveling of the economic playing field for our British planters challenged by the Brazilian and other South American planters, and the other intangibles needed to sustain our great empire. Is he nuts? Actually, we need more bloody Maroon wars and African and Creole slave rebellions. Then we will be forced to sue for peace and abolish slavery. The ex-slaves and Maroons, in turn, will become our vassals and allies. Thereafter, we will get on to the bloody business at hand—building a greater British Empire."

Later, I contacted Colonel Henriques to inquire about the Maroons and to plan a raid on the plantation of the Honorable Albert Pike. I decided to kill him and to orchestrate a chain of slave uprisings and Maroon attacks throughout the island. The objective was to escalate the pressure on the Jamaican colony to accept Dr. Brown's agenda as its active policy.

On our way to the village of the blind voodoo priestess, Colonel Henriques told me about the First Maroon War (1730–1739), which forced the Redcoats to sue for peace with the Maroon leader Cudjoe. They signed peace agreements. Cudjoe agreed to return new slave escapees to the Redcoats and to assist the Redcoats in future slave rebellions. His sister Nanny (the Maroon version of the Celtic warrior queen Boudicca) thought Cudjoe had betrayed the Africans and the Creoles. Unflappably, she believed the Maroons should wage a total war for unconditional freedom or death. Courageously, she broke off from the talks and fought (with voodoo and guerilla warfare) the Redcoats until she and her forces were annihilated and her village was leveled. It became a cemetery plot. The survivors of her village, considered a threat to the colonial security, were exiled to Nova Scotia, where they were enlisted in a Maroon militia to fight against warring Native Indians. After the Indian Wars, still fearing the Maroons' pride and independence, the redcoats shipped them to Sierra Leone, Africa. As for Nanny, the Redcoats dragged her body around the countryside and town squares to refute the myth and the legend of Nanny of the Maroons—she had claimed voodoo made her invincible to bullets. The display of her body in the marketplaces quelled the other Maroon holdouts. Grudgingly, they joined Cudjoe at the peace summit convened by the Redcoats, and Cudjoe and the British general exchanged hats to symbolize the end of the First Maroon War.

The legacy of the peace treaty in 1739 had a negative effect on future revolts. For example, in 1760, Tacky, a Coromantee chief in Africa, led a slave rebellion. He was an able leader who led a successful campaign against the planters (and their families) and two companies of regular troops. The tide began to turn against Tacky's forces after the governor called upon the Scott's Hall Maroons (they were bound by the 1739 peace treaty, and they were given additional incentives, including greater autonomy) to assist the Redcoats. One of Tacky's lieutenants (mostly obeah men) was hanged to disprove his claim that he could not be killed. Davey—a Maroon and an elite sharpshooter—shot Tacky in the back when he was fleeing through the forest. Cornered in a cave, thirteen of the late Tacky's lieutenants committed suicide rather than surrender to the Redcoats and their allies. For the next few months, scattered rebels continued to fight in the mountains against the Redcoats and the Maroons (the allies). Indomitably, they fought to the death or committed suicide. They lived by the mottos "Fight or die" and "Freedom or death." Favorably, Lady History will honor them as heroes who rose to the challenge in their gravest hour—when Mother Africa needed them to fight and die as men for her honor.

In the end, the Redcoats exiled Maroon sympathizers and African and Creole "troublemaking" slaves to Haiti and other destinations. A few Maroon forces continued to break the 1739 peace treaty. In turn, the Redcoats imported Cuban dogs and Brazilian bounty hunters, who were killed or failed in their pursuit of the Maroons. The Maroons were talented guerrilla fighters. They were able to blend into their surroundings with superb camouflage (both visual and auditory disguises—bird calls), and they trapped their enemies (men or dogs) with highly tactical ambushes. They were masters of the art of stealth.

Finally, we arrived at the Maroon village. We were greeted at our carriage. We were led to a festive celebration and a magnificent feast. We enjoyed the traditional dances, songs, and meal. Maroon cuisine is similar to kosher and halal cuisines. For example, they eschew pork and other forbidden food. In addition, cattle and chicken are ritually butchered. Colonel Henriques suspended his taste as he dug into his meal—he was used to eating nonkosher food in his line of work. The Maroon cuisine is an acquired taste, but our food was superbly prepared and presented at the banquet.

At the end of the festivities, I conspired with the elders of the village about the preemptive strike against the Honorable Albert Pike's plantation. I provided the layout of the plantation. I ordered that the slaves should be freed; that the judge, his family, and the white overseers should be killed; and that Dr. Brown and I should be taken for ransom (including but not limited to social demands and the return of political prisoners). I spelled out the strategic demands that they should stipulate for the ransom. In any case, the Redcoats would meet some of the demands and counterstrike against the Maroons. Thus, they would provide the Maroons with the pretext to launch the Second Maroon War, the mother of all wars to capture the island of Jamaica—to transform it into "the Base" or "Ground Zero," from which we could export the Jamaican Revolution to Haiti, Cuba, the rest of the Caribbean, Central America, South America, North America, and the world. The Jamaican Revolution would provide the exodus (warpath) from Babylon (slavery) to Zion (world domination—to secure our freedom—after all, the Romans built their empire via a series of "defensive" and "preemptive" wars). Feverishly, I wanted my war of liberation—to return Mother Africa to her imperial throne and to return the world as her imperial footstool. Verily, I was ready to be the sacrificial lamb to bring salvation to my beloved African people.

At the conclusion of our powwow, the elders passed around a cup containing a concoction made of rum, gunpowder, graveyard dirt, and their own blood. They drank to seal the oath for the warpath we planned to unleash on the Redcoats. However, I feigned sipping the brew. I wasn't going to drink it, nor did I want to insult my hosts by a blatant refusal. The blind chieftainess escorted me to my carriage. She kissed me on both of my cheeks, and she warned, "My lord! Wear your amulet because it will save you from bullets at the age of thirty-six—delivered by spies sent by the United States."

I smiled as I boarded the carriage and pondered the following thoughts of a new Africa. In my new Africa, I would lobby for the illegality of voodoo and paganism—their gods are demonic forces and not forces of our Lord. The new Africa would be a modernized and a Westernized empire. The empire would be supported by the four pillars of science, technology, reason, and monotheism (mainly of a Christian character). The monotheistic religion would accommodate Christianity, Judaism, and Islam. We would foster a secular society. Mercilessly, we would repress militant Islam, militant Zionism, and Christian sects (I would be the judge of its definition under God) that would threaten the empire or the United States of Africa. We would return Palestine (Israel) to the Jews and Jerusalem to them as their capital city. In turn, Israel would be a vassal state of the African Empire. We would not fulfill the old Zionist vision of a Jewish empire stretching "from the Nile to the Euphrates." In addition, we would make sure that militant Zionists wouldn't create a fifth column in support of our enemies and competitors in our empire. We would have to accommodate the Arabs and the Moslems because Mother Africa (northern) was their home, too. Africa would be of a Christian character because of my belief in Jesus Christ as the Creator of mankind. Africa Proper would encompass Asia Minor, Southeast Asia (including the East Indies), the subcontinent of India, part of the Ottoman Turkish Empire, part of the Austrian Empire, part of the Russian Empire, Australia, Madagascar, New Zealand, and Antarctica. Greater Africa would encompass the whole world in due time via the pen of diplomacy and the sword of war. Ink and blood would create and maintain our empire. The capital of the renewed empire would be in Egypt, where "the Kings of the South"—Libyans (Arabs), Persians (non-Arabic Muslims), and Ethiopians (sub-Saharan and Black Africans)—would govern under a neo-pharaoh (a black pharaoh of a Christian yet secular character).

The following week, we dined at Judge Albert Pike's mansion. The dinner was impeccably served with pomp and circumstance. Indeed, the good judge enjoyed his last meal in an entertainment/gourmet extravaganza setting. In intoxication, the judge began to discuss the dinner's agenda. He scolded, "We need to explore final solutions to our Maroon problem and Jewish problem. The Maroons need to be completely exterminated from Jamaica. Likewise, the Jews need to be expelled from Jamaica because they have continued to trade with the Maroons by selling arms and other essential supplies to our enemy. In audacity, they are lobbying Kingston and London for the right to be planters and owners of slaves. I fear they might sell us out. Let's not forget, they betrayed Spain. After all, they are parasites and bloodsuckers who feed on their hosts—until death—and move on to new hosts to continue their bloodletting enterprise. For God's sake, they have their hands in the sugar and slave trades, banking, newspapers and similar publications, insurance, education, shipping, merchant, legal, and other vital industries. So I say, let's pass legislation and institute ethnic cleansing policies to eradicate the Maroons once and for all and gradually expel the Jews from Jamaica! We have historical precedence on our side, according to an encyclopedia, and I quote: 'Jews were expelled from England in 1290, France in 1306, Hungary from 1349 to 1360, Provence in 1394 and 1490, Austria in 1421, Spain after the Reconquista, Portugal in 1497, Russia in 1724, and from various parts of Germany at various times.' End of quote. In one stroke, we'll get rid of a bunch of scavengers, the Maroons; and pests, the Jews—wild animals, the Maroons; and vermin, the Jews."

In an explosion of temper and disgust, Dr. John Brown violently pounded the table, frightening the other dinner guests. Perspiration cascaded from his forehead, and frothy spittle spurted out of his mouth. He bloodcurdlingly screamed, "Your Honor! You might disparage my character! It's your right under freedom of speech to do so! But I have to correct you on your remarks on the Jews. Let's ignore the virulent anti-Semitism of your comments. Blatantly, it's obvious that you're an unabashed anti-Semite. Howbeit, I cannot ignore the truth.

"To the world—divided by Spain and Portugal with the blessing of the Vatican—Great Britain was a rogue nation of pirates, buccaneers, high-seas robbers, and barbarians in the New World. A rogue nation bent on destroying— dominating—the twin towers of colonization, Spain and Portugal. Thanks to the Jews! In the last century, they began to transform us into an empire of wealth and a country of law and order. They introduced the technology of sugar to us. They financed our fledgling enterprises. They switched their alliances to us after we promised them that we would respect their inalienable right to practice their religion without persecution. They manage the plantations of our many absentee landlords. They act as the middlemen who facilitate the smooth operation of our empire. Oliver Cromwell welcomed them with open arms. He was the greater beneficiary of the Anglo-Jewish Alliance. We will not be able to compensate them for their collective service to the empire. Without the Jews, England wouldn't be the superpower it is today. You referred to the Jews as parasites and vermin! I categorically disagree with your viewpoints. The Jews are producers! They are like the fertilized and watered rich soil that enables our beloved empire to grow and to prosper. At best, we are as guilty as the Jews for their preconceived sins. At worst, we are guiltier, based on empirical evidence.

"You talked about the Jews lobbying to become planters and owners of slave estates. Let's not forget, they are awarded equal status, as planters and slave owners, in Brazil and in Surinam. I do not endorse their lobby—I equally do not support the non-Jewish lobby, too—because I'm an avowed abolitionist for reasons given in my published book and other publications at Oxford University. Again, with due respect, I have to rabidly defend the honor of a good people— the Jews, great contributors to Great Britain.

"In regard to the Maroons, I will not endorse genocide or war-criminal activities. We are in agreement that the Maroons are a thorn in our side. However, we have to think of better solutions. After all, the empire is built and held buoyant on the backs of slavery. Slavery is the foundation on which the great house of our empire is erected. The Maroons are the ones who assisted us in the suppression of Tacky's Slave Rebellion in 1760. Unfortunately, we have to weed out the tares from among the wheat. Let's not burn the whole field to kill a few tares. The latter mode of attack would be foolish and wasteful. Besides, we have to set an example for the slaves and free blacks who live and work among us. The right example of a civilized society to the inferior civilizations of our world—we are the Romans to the world's barbarians. For example, Lieutenant Afrika Kenjo von Kunhardt rose from the shackles of slavery to be dining at your table while we discussed our service to our king and to our country."

Retired Chief Judge Albert Pike angrily but calmly countered, "How dare you insult me in my house, and in front of my family and my domestic slaves? At best, you are a misguided nigger and *Ikey Mo* lover," he said, using the British nickname for Jews. "At worse, you are a self-hating Briton, and you're in the deep pockets of Jewish lobbyists. At worst, you are a traitor to the British Empire, for which you feign devoted loyalty. I want you to depart with your pet monkey," he said, pointing at me. "Now! In the morning, I will contact my close friend General Kevin Kirk Kinsley to request a transfer on your behalf. I want you to be expelled from Jamaica. Jamaica is a conservative institution. Preach your liberalism at Oxford University, not in my Jamaica!"

We rose to depart from the table, but we were precluded when all hell broke loose. The Maroons were raiding. Quickly, they overcame the defenses of the plantation. I stopped Dr. Brown from resistance by exclaiming, "Don't fight back! I have a feeling they are going to negotiate a ransom for us!"

Immediately, he realized I was involved in the unfolding massacre.

The good judge valiantly fought to save his family and property. In the end, his last stand proved fruitless. The Maroons hung his warm body on a Union Jack flagpole under the words, "We will fight or die for our FREEDOM! Long Live Mother Africa! Death to the 1739 Peace Treaty! Death to the Redcoats! Courtesy of the Maroons!" They freed the slaves, killed a few loyal domestic slaves, and took the good doctor and me as captives.

Predictably, they exchanged us to the Redcoats for a ransom and political prisoners. Furiously, General Williamson, the new governor of Jamaica, demanded a counterattack. Later, Sir Kevin Kirk Kinsley (newly knighted by King George III) raced back to Jamaica upon learning the news. Suspiciously, I was given the cold shoulder by my white colleagues in the British Intelligence Service. In the absence of Sir Kevin Kirk Kinsley, I was under the protection of my godfather. Dr. Brown saw to it that he covered my tracks and collaboration with the Maroons. Afterward, he counseled, "You are a cold and calculating contriver! But, thank God, you are my cold and calculating contriver," he said, borrowing the phrase, loosely, from a popular politician. "Please, do not execute similar plans in the future without my express consent. May the good judge rest in peace; he got what he rightfully deserved. Good job…my black beast!

"I want to send you to Haiti because I don't want Sir Kevin Kirk Kinsley to interview you about the recent Maroon incident. I'll take care of him. Moreover, Haiti is ripe for a slave revolution because of the present French Revolution. I want you to contact Dutty Boukman—an exiled Maroon in Haiti. He will teach you the ropes and the culture of Haiti. Don't worry about Jamaica; Colonel Henriques and I will supervise the undermining of slavery in Jamaica. His Majesty needs your service to bring Haiti into the fold of his expanding empire."

He was semicorrect—Mother Africa needed my service to bring Haiti (and the world) into the fold of her renewed empire. I departed, transported by the *Hamita*, Colonel Henriques's merchant ship, for Haiti to see the Jamaican-born Maroon Dutty Boukman. For the last time, I departed—after my promotion to captain of His Majesty's Secret Service—the beautiful island of Jamaica, the cradle of the rebirth of Mother Africa.

*Nanny the Maroon—sister to other **great Maroon leaders** such as*
*Cudjoe, Accompong, Cuffy, Quao, and **Paro**. Throughout the 1700s,*
*they fought the Redcoats to a standstill **on the island of Jamaica**.*

Source: http://www.jamaica-gleaner.com/pages/history/
story0012.html

9

IGNITING THE HAITIAN REVOLUTION

DURING MY VOYAGE, I read *The Interesting Narrative of the Life of Olaudah Equiano, or Gustavus Vassa the African* (1789), written by my associate Olaudah Equiano. My interest was drawn to one of his poems.

A Poem
By Olaudah Equiano, 1789
Well may I say my life has been
One scene of sorrow and pain;
From early days I griefs have known,
And as I grew my griefs have grown.

Dangers were always in my path,
And fear of wrath and sometimes death;
While pale dejection in me reign'd
I often wept, my grief constrain'd.

When taken from my native land,
By an unjust and cruel band,
How did uncommon dread prevail!
My sighs no more I could conceal.

Although it is a powerfully abolitionist autobiography, it is too proreform and seeks its audience in the British ruling class. I decided my autobiography would seek its audience in the African revolutionary class; therefore, it would be a prorevolutionary autobiography.

Furthermore, I read my correspondence from Captain J. G. Stedman. He informed me he was writing a book entitled *Narrative of a Five Years' Expedition against the Revolted Negroes of Surinam*, based on his military service in Surinam. He believed it would be published in 1796.

After reading the captain's correspondence, I turned my attention to a book written by Dr. Wladyslaw Roczniak III entitled *The Greatest Holocaust Ever: The Evil of the Western Civilization*. Dr. Roczniak III was a Polish adventurer, an atheist, a freemason, a Francophile, and a trained historian and philosopher. He was a close ally of Maximilien Robespierre, Marshal Aristide (Wladyslaw was one of his Polish agents), François-Noël Babeuf (a.k.a. Gracchus Babeuf), Jean Paul Marat, Filippo Giuseppe Maria Ludovico Buonarroti (a.k.a. Philippe Buonarroti), and Tadeusz Kosciuszko (a veteran of the American Revolutionary War and the commander in chief of all of the Polish forces during the Kosciuszko Uprising, which took place in Poland in 1794). In my opinion, Dr. Roczniak was one of the greatest writers in history. I endeavored to model my writing style after his eloquent and lucid writing skills—and, to a lesser extent, Thomas Clarkson's writing style, displayed in his 1786 essay that was published as "An essay on the slavery and commerce of the human species, particularly the African, translated from a Latin Dissertation," which was honored with the first prize at the University of Cambridge for the year 1785 (he won a BA competition and was the first person to win an MA competition as well).

According to secondary accounts, Dr. Roczniak was drawn to the suffering of the African and Creole slaves while he was visiting a friend in Haiti. Quickly, he became sympathetic to the slaves and was transformed into a present-day Bartholomew de la Casa. For five years, he conducted intensive research for his book while living in Hispaniola. He interviewed people—slaves, slave merchants and owners, and others—with personal experience of slavery and the slave trade. Subsequently, he published his uncompromising book based upon his thorough and exhaustive research. He reported, "The stolen and raped

Africans, on the slave ships via the Atlantic passage, were as if in a liminal space, preceding the life of slavery or sort of like the gates to Hell." In a blatant, graphic, and shocking style (as if to shock his readers with the unvarnished truth of slavery—particularly the mid-Atlantic slave trade), he described the games that were played with the human bounty—how the men were whipped and how the women were raped.

Dr. Roczniak continued to illustrate the brutality of the voyage taken by slave ships in the mid-Atlantic passage. He explicitly utilized symbolism such as, "The slave ship is similar to a wooden coffin that ends the life of a free man or an artificial womb that then expels from its innards a slave."

According to rumors, Robespierre wept upon reading the book and sought out the Polish doctor. In turn, Dr. Roczniak persuaded Robespierre to use his influence to ban slavery during the French Revolution. He was unable to persuade Robespierre to assist, effectively, his compatriot Tadeusz Kosciuszko in his uprising for the liberty of Poland. Sadly, twenty thousand Polish revolutionaries were eventually massacred in one day, and Dr. Roczniak wrote a book: *Polish Liberation: Make It Happen.*

He turned to Marshal Aristide also. However, the marshal was precluded from assisting his valued agent by the governing body (influenced by Robespierre) of Revolutionary France despite the courage and distinction Polish units projected while fighting alongside the French revolutionary armies during the campaigns of the 1790s. As a matter of fact, the French Revolution was successful partly because Prussian troops were tied down in Poland during the Kosciuszko Uprising. Russian and Austrian troops were distracted by the Polish threat on their borders and internal instability also. Revolutionary France failed to be the buffer or counterbalance to Prussia, Austria, and Russia that would have allowed Poland to defend the integrity of its borders, to regain the independence of the Polish nation, and to strengthen universal liberties (as proposed by Andrzej Tadeusz Bonawentura Kościuszko).

In 1794, Dr. Roczniak was guillotined with his ally, Robespierre. Marshal Aristide attempted to rescue his able Polish agent, but he was unable to overcome the resistance of Robespierre's political enemies. In the end, the Marshal wasn't willing "to stick his neck out" for his Polish friend. The marshal threatened to resign upon Dr. Roczniak's murder, but his political allies—Talleyrand and Joseph Fouché—counseled him to withdraw his resignation.

Going back to Dr. Roczniak's masterpiece *The Greatest Holocaust Ever: The Evil of Western Civilization*, he discussed the consequences of slavery. He stated:

> The future of the Africans will be at a crossroad or will be like a double-edged sword. In comparison, we noticed the Jews are able to evolve into a stronger race (collectively) because of the persecutions, pogroms and anti-Semitism they overcame throughout the centuries. Thus, the Jewish descendants adapted via nature (hereditary traits) and nurture (the Jewish mentality) for their continued survival in our world. In addition, we noticed the descendants of Pilgrims and Puritans who fled Western Europe because of religious persecution are able to evolve into a stronger nation (collectively as Americans). As a matter of fact, the Americans will continue to get stronger (via hereditary traits and the environment) as they expand westward (displacing Native Americans, in the process, for good or ill).
>
> Like the American nation and the Jews (whose trials and tribulations are very pale in comparison to the Holocaust of the Black race), African slaves will be able to overcome their station and unrivaled oppression. However, they need a messiah who will be able to create and execute a vision and ideology (even if the messiah's life should be terminated, prematurely) to motivate the masses. They cannot wait for their total freedom to be given to them as a gift. Nope, they have to earn their total freedom as a prize. Likewise, serfs, peasants and commoners (the Third Estate) have to earn their freedom from the aristocratic and clerical classes 'by whatever means necessary.' The nobility will not voluntarily give 'freedom' to the lower classes.
>
> On the other hand, if the African and Creole slaves (even if they were to be physically emancipated) fail to aggressively grab the prize on their own—they will be doomed to be the backward, regressive and apathetic race (mired in mental slavery) of our world. The preceding is the crossroad (or the double-edged sword) the Africans will have to

choose which path to take—the path to a racial Heaven or the path to a racial Hell. They choose not for themselves alone but for their children's future—the future of their race.

Like Robespierre, I wept upon reading Dr. Roczniak's great work. Better yet, I had an epiphany. My childhood memories (which I tried to block) of the Mid-Atlantic Passage broke through my psychological dam. When I was a child, I suffered many sleepless nights dominated by nightmares, cold sweats, and gnashing of teeth. I tried to overcome my trauma via a split personality. I developed an alter ego in an attempt to retake control over my emotions and destiny. I masked my pain (like a violently raped little girl trying to heal and cleanse herself of her ordeal) with charisma, education, and the dream to motivate my people to climb the evolutionary ladder to ultimate freedom. Now I'm a grown adult who is aiming to grab his prize on behalf of his people.

Alas, Eurocentric history might paint me as an unlikable character who was a ruthless murderer bent on a genocidal war that placed one race over another race. To my critics I say, "Genocidal war is as much a part of Western civilization as missionary work!" Besides, we would write our own history as long as we won the Great War I was about to ignite in Saint-Domingue. Verily, I might be prematurely slain despite the pagan prophecy of my imperial rule. For the record, I was a Christian and an educated individual who was not a believer in voodoo (although it has its political use as it pertains to the control of the masses, like what Napoleon said of religion) and other superstitious relics of an unenlightened era. Thus, the message (vision and ideology) is greater than the messenger because whereas the messenger is mortal, the message should be immortal. Toussaint L'Ouverture (whom I will later discuss) put it best: "In overthrowing me, you have cut only the trunk of the tree of liberty. It will spring again from the roots for they are numerous and deep."

Finally, I landed in Saint-Domingue, Haiti—the land of my fate and destiny, and perhaps the destiny (the beginning of their journey to freedom) of my African race. On my way to see Dutty Boukman, my guides informed me of the death of Vincent Ogé (a Haitian mulatto who lived in Paris, London, and New York City) and his friend Jean-Baptiste Chavannes. They had formed a revolutionary group of slaves and mulattoes. The group (inspired by the French Revolution) defeated the National Guard in a defensive battle. Finally, the group was defeated by regular troops (three times the number of the National Guard and almost four times the number of the revolutionary group) armed with artillery. Ogé and Chavannes were extradited from the Spanish part of the island. After a trial, the two comrades were sentenced to death via an excruciating medieval method—death on the wheel (on February 25, 1791). The rest of the rank and file were hung or sentenced to imprisonment. Twenty-one of their adherents were hung and another thirty sentenced to another ancient and medieval punishment—the galleys. Monsieur Ogé had been a recruit and an operative of the ubiquitous Dr. John Brown.

Finally, I was introduced to the Jamaican-born Maroon Dutty Boukman, of Dahomian descent. He was an avowed obeah man (voodoo priest). I realized it would be best to reach the slave masses via a church or a temple. It is the best forum to arouse the masses to action. He was equally eloquent in the Jamaican and Haitian Creole. I spoke with him in French. Monsieur Boukman comprehended French, English, Spanish, Jamaican Creole, and Haitian Creole. He was a great communicator. Finally, I laid out my plan and gave him a ring from his sister in Jamaica. He embraced me and confided that he had dreamed of my arrival. After the warm greetings, we started to carefully organize the revolution.

Boukman ignited the Haitian Revolution before I had completely organized the rebellion. Worse, I was still waiting for smuggled logistics and supplies from Jamaica. On August 14, 1791, Boukman spurred his followers to revolt while chanting, "Live free or die!" He told his followers that he could not be killed by the French because he was protected by the voodoo gods and ancestors.

I scrambled to bail water out of the sinking ship. Alas, it was too late. I had to make rapid adjustments in order to salvage the liberation of Mother Africa. At first, Boukman, surrounded by a cadre of battle-hardened Jamaican Maroon exiles and Haitian slaves, got the best of the white population. He created a bloody trail of white bodies and burned plantations. Eventually, the planters organized a vengeful counterstrike. In turn, they created a bloody puddle of black bodies and destruction in Cap-Haïtien. Bravely, Boukman and his Jamaican Maroons fought to their deaths on Oct. 15, 1791, on the outskirts of Cap-Haïtien. The

French authority advertised their false claims to immortality on pikes in the Place d'Armes of Cap. Like King Leonidas of the three hundred Spartans legend, Boukman's head was placed on a pike in the square. Luckily, I salvaged the situation by sending agents to stir up rebellions throughout Haiti. I was successful in this, but my disguise as a Haitian slave was uncovered by the French. I was arrested and sentenced to death as a spy. However, I produced an official document depicting me as an undercover agent for the French Intelligence Service under the supervision of General Aristide. Grudgingly, they released me and swamped me with the utmost apologies. Cunningly, I forgave them while I appreciated my charmed life. To myself, I swore to rescue victory out of the jaws of defeat and to see the revolution to its successful end—world domination—the freedom of Mother Africa.

First, I had to deal with the complications of the early revolution—internal battles between French Republic Loyalists, White Royalists, Negroes, and mulattoes. Worse yet, French troops departing from France to Haiti while British (from Jamaica) and Spanish (from Cuba) expeditionary forces sailed to Haiti. Worse yet, I needed a Haitian native leader to replace Boukman—a Haitian George Washington I could rally the troops around (I am at my best working behind the scenes—the power behind the throne—the brain behind the strong man).

I found my George Washington in the person of Pierre François Dominique Toussaint. History recorded his name as Toussaint L'Ouverture (a man of overtures). At first, L'Ouverture was a Royalist and a reluctant warrior. After he saved and shipped his master and his family to Baltimore, Maryland, he joined the revolution to remedy the poor treatment the Negroes suffered under the whites and the mulattoes.

Over the years, L'Ouverture (as an ally of Spain) fought against the French after she repealed the citizenship of free Negroes in her dominions in 1791. Then he (as an ally of France) fought against the British and Spanish expeditionary forces (after France abolished slavery in 1793). He fought against the mulatto forces under the command of Riguad and Alexander Sabes Petion in 1800. He had won every battle (with the help of diseases decimating the enemies) at that point. He was called the ghost warrior because of his ubiquitous ability during the military campaigns. In his heart, L'Ouverture was a French Loyalist. He wanted autonomy under French rule. He wanted Haiti to be a respected vassal of France rather than an independent and sovereign nation. L'Ouverture's top lieutenants (whom I will discuss later), General Jean-Jacques Dessalines and General Henry Christophe, and I disagreed with him. However, the pros of his ideology outweighed the cons in the earlier campaigns. Reluctantly, we tolerated his political platform. We could not afford to be divided while we were fighting against the odds by trying to change history—attempting the impossible. Unity and military discipline were our strength.

In the interim, France promoted L'Ouverture to the ranks of general and lieutenant governor of Haiti. He consolidated his power and became the leader of Hispaniola when he invaded Santa Domingo (the capital of the Spanish parts of the Island). He set the slaves free and was given the constitutional title of governor general for life, in exchange for allowing Santa Domingo to govern itself under local autonomy.

In due time, I became the general of the Haitian Military Intelligence. I trained and drilled an elite guard to form the Republican Guard. They were quantitatively inferior to the Haitian regular troops, but they were qualitatively superior in training and equipment. They provided bodyguards, secret police, spies, intelligence officers, military police, elite troops, special-interest troops (e.g., military scientists), and special-service troops for the Haitian Revolution. The motto of the Republican Guard was inspired by Boukman: "Live free or die!" They operated as an elite paramilitary unit independent of the regular Haitian troops. They were the best fighters during the revolution.

Plus, I developed a youth division of the Republican Guard called the Boukman Youth. Partly, the Boukman Youth was inspired by the Ashanti initiation of youth into manhood and the rigorous and austere training of the selected youth into the secret Black Panther Society of Orego, my ancestral home. In the end, they were malleable and obedient to their superiors. We taught them to be benevolent to their friends but to be harsh with their enemies and themselves. We were creating black Roman soldiers and black Spartan soldiers for the future. I chose an exiled Maroon warrior to be their leader. In addition, I collected in-depth dossiers on everyone (important friends and foes) I knew in the world.

In 1798, I tried to instigate the Third Maroon War (in Jamaica) due to the successes we were enjoying in Haiti. The Second Maroon War had ended in defeat for the Maroons (they were deceived into a conditional surrender by false promises), but they had not given up the struggle. I smuggled spies via my connections with Colonel Henriques and Dr. Brown to the parish of Trelawny. They were able to set off an uprising of its slaves. Howbeit, Governor Edward Trelawny put down the uprising using elite regular troops. Governor Trelawny tried to assuage the fears of the colonists of an impending Jamaican revolution. There were rumors of Haitian operatives organizing rebellions throughout Jamaica. To counter the fears, he arrested two of my Haitian spies on the charge of conspiracy. He fatally tortured one while another was hanged, but they did not provide key intelligence to the Redcoats. Notwithstanding, Governor Trelawny and Sir Kevin Kirk Kinsley continued to conspire with exiled white French Royalists to capture Haiti for the British Crown.

Getting back to the Haitian Washingtonian figure in the form of General L'Ouverture, he alarmed the French government (dominated by Napoleon Bonaparte) when he became the singular leader of the island of Hispaniola. Napoleon feared a declaration of independence from Haiti. He did not want to risk losing the strategic island, where he was planning an invasion of North America (he planned to link with French forces in Louisiana). In 1802, the French minister of the Public Treasury, Francois Barbe-Marbois; the French foreign minister Charles Talleyrand; the head of the Secret Police, Joseph Fouche; and the head of Military Intelligence, Marshal Aristide (newly promoted) urged Napoleon to send his brother-in-law, General Leclerc, at the head of a fleet of warships and soldiers (a mixture of Poles, Swiss, Haitian mulattoes, and regular French troops) to subdue our leader. Toussaint faced an armada of seventy warships and twenty-five thousand battle-hardened troops—the best in the world.

Toussaint ferociously fought the French and a Haitian mulatto force commanded by Alexander Sabes Petion (I will discuss him later). On May 1, 1802, he approved the capitulation of his generals, overriding Dessalines and me. Yet again, Toussaint's French Loyalist ideals overruled common sense. Dessalines and I recognized that we needed a Napoleonic figure instead of a Washingtonian figure. We needed an autocratic leader and not a democratic leader. We needed a leader who would match the ruthlessness of our opponent—Napoleon Bonaparte.

Adding salt to injury, Toussaint was tricked into captivity by the French. He was taken to France as a common criminal. Toussaint's dismissed generals mobilized to respond to the new developments. Below are the profiles of Toussaint's top generals.

Firstly, General Dessalines was a ruthless racist—he hated white people. He and his adjunct, Boisrond-Tonnerre, designed a plan for genocide (involving my fanatical Republican Guard) against whites. I intervened and mitigated their proposed final solution to the white problem to the best of my ability. After the death of Toussaint, he was able to execute most of his plan. Ironically, he retained his former white slave master (the former owner of the Crown Hotel) as his butler. I understand his extreme hatred for whites. The scars on his back are a tattooed memento of the agony he experienced as a slave. He designed the Haitian flag by ripping the white (symbolizing the white race) out of the Tricolor and replacing it with the Haitian coat of arms. (My idea for the Imperial African flag is red [our blood], white [our enlightenment], and black [our people], with a symbol denoting the Kenjonian character for the number thirteen [Kenjonian symbolism]).

Secondly, General Boisrond-Tonnerre is the father of the Haitian Act of Independence. He wanted to pen the original document on a parchment made from white skin. Once more, I (with the help of General Petion and General Christophe) overruled him, and he authored the sacred writing on the appropriate paper. Compromisingly, we did not alter the style and the content of his final draft. The Act of Independence portrayed the implacableness of the writer—vindictive and sublime in all its glory. General Dessalines was extremely delighted with the final draft. Tonnerre was the best friend of Dessalines. They were different in physique and education, but they were bonded by their Europhobic passion.

Thirdly, Petion was a fellow alumnus of Ecole Militaire. After his defeat in 1800 by Toussaint, he was spirited out of Haiti by Marshal Aristide to study military tactics and munitions. He was recruited in the French Intelligence by the Marshal, too. However, Dessalines and I were able to persuade him to join our cause. Petion's love of his country overcame his mulatto background. He was instrumental in the final defeat of the French. Haiti is indebted to his greatness and his decision.

Fourthly, Henry Christophe was a man of ambition and dignity, which befitted his 6'11" frame (which dwarfed my 6'4" frame). He was an exile from the British colony of Saint Christopher in the Lesser Antilles (hence his surname). He proclaimed to me that he would commit suicide rather than surrender to the French. At all times, he kept a silver bullet in his possession. The silver bullet would be his way out in case he was cornered. I showed him the best way to shoot himself (orally) to ensure a painless and swift death. He didn't want to imitate the failed attempt of the French Jacobin Robespierre (the Prince of Terror) to commit suicide.

These were the men left to decide the fate of the Haitian Revolution after the exile of Toussaint. Immediately, I left for France to bring back our symbol of the Revolution via my contact with Marshal Aristide. Dessalines, Petion, and Christophe returned to the battlefield. In the end, General Leclerc and his troops were decimated by disease and the ingenious leadership of Dessalines. Other French generals such as Rochambeau (who was captured by British troops) were defeated by Dessalines and unsung heroes such as Jeanne Marie, the wife of Brigade Commander Lamartiniere. She was our Haitian Joan of Arc.

In France, I met with Marshal Aristide. He informed me of Napoleon's reluctance to release Toussaint. He was able to provide for my protection only. He introduced me to the French minister of the Public Treasury, Francois Barbe-Marbois; the French Foreign minister Charles Talleyrand; the head of the Secret Police, Joseph Fouche; and Napoleon. He presented me as a veteran French Intelligence operative. He informed Napoleon that I shared his birthday (I was born on August 15, 1769) and that I was an alumnus of his alma mater.

Napoleon was dismissive and condescending to me. Napoleon was a racist, like most white men of our time. However, he was a moderate racist because Napoleon considered himself to be a super genius—an uber genius who was in a class by himself, the genius who views other humans as his vassals and inferiors, regardless of their rank—the Pope, emperors, kings, peasants, serfs, and slaves. He believed he would be the greatest military genius of all time. Thus, I had to eschew personalizing his slight because Napoleon treated everyone with equal disdain.

Then I went to visit Général Thomas-Alexandre Dumas. The general was born in Haiti, on 25 March 1762. He was a son of Antoine-Alexandre Davy, marquis de la Pailleterie, chevalier de Saint-Louis (a nobleman with the artillery), and a slave, Marie-Césette Dumas. He was a great general who was celebrated in his homeland of Haiti. He was a "brother" who was ruined by Napoleon because of allegations that he had been involved in a plot to overthrow Napoleon during the Egyptian campaigns. In Egypt, he had been Napoleon's right-hand man and had led a cavalry divided into four brigades. The brigades were commanded by Leclerc, Murat, Mireur, and Davout, respectively. In turn, they were direct reports of General Dumas.

I met his wife and his infant son. We spoke about the good old days. He told me about an incident in his youth of a fellow mulatto born into French nobility. They were in a salon when the fellow started to brag about his ancestry. Then he started to negate Dumas's maternal ancestry. Defensively, he responded, "I might have descended from monkeys, but it is obvious your esteemed ancestry devolved into a monkey!" The salon was in an uproar with laughter. The mulatto demanded a duel, but the fellow feigned sickness on the appointed day. In response, Dumas sent a note to him that read, "I wish you a speedy recovery from your yellow fever, and don't forget to drink your chicken soup and eat lots of yellow bananas."

Plus, we discussed the American Revolution, the French Revolution, and the Haitian Revolution. He, a staunch Republican, asked me about the type of government and type of economy we would establish in Haiti. I told him it was going to be a little individualism/capitalism and a little collectivism/socialism. I described the type of government in further detail.

In addition, General Dumas told me that Napoleon had used cannons to bombard the nose of the sphinx because of its Negroid features. He had challenged Napoleon's order to destroy historical artifacts. In retaliation, Napoleon began to plot his demise. I gave the honorable general some money because he was penniless (a victim of Napoleon's wrath) and gravely ill.

In 1803, Toussaint was murdered (via neglect and starvation) in prison, and Napoleon was forced to sell Louisiana because he was losing Haiti as a potential launching pad for his troops into the Greater Caribbean and North America. I was allowed to return to Haiti under the condition I would attempt to return Haiti to French rule. I broke my promise upon my arrival in Haiti. I vowed I would repay Napoleon, in kind, for his treatment of the Haitian heroes Toussaint and Dumas.

I informed Dessalines of the death of our beloved leader. I advised, "Our Washington, Toussaint, was cowardly murdered, but our Napoleon, Dessalines, is born today. You have to lead us to final victory. Death to the French and to white men! Amen!"

On January 1, 1804, Haiti became an independent nation—the first black republic in the world and the second independent nation in the New World (following the United States).

Dessalines promoted me to the rank of marshal upon his declaration. I was concerned about his security. I designed a tight security network around him, and I argued with him to follow my security protocols. In turn, he would share his dissatisfaction as it pertained to my lack of a security detail around me. I replied, "Death comes to me by fate. I will die via destiny's design." I would ride to the headquarters by myself or drawn in a carriage with a driver only.

An old nemesis was taking note of my lack of security also. General Dick Elliott had returned on the scene. He was invited to the White House for a meeting with President Thomas Jefferson and Alexander Hamilton (who had cast the decisive vote in the controversial presidential election of Jefferson and who was killed in a duel later). General Elliott reported, "Mr. President and Mr. Hamilton, I recommend we activate Operation Black Fox, based on intelligence gathered about a threat in Haiti—Marshal Afrika Kenjo von Kunhardt. He is the most singular threat to our young republic. He is public enemy number one. According to my sources, he has evidence that you have black ancestry. He wants to use the information to blackmail or bribe you during your political campaigns. He has designed backup plans for the assassinations of Napoleon, the king and prime minister of Britain, the governor of Jamaica, and you—Mr. President. He is training volunteers from his Republican Guard for suicide assassination missions in which they will pose as slaves or freemen to get close to their targets. He is dispersing Republican Guard operatives to other countries to instigate slave uprisings.

"Since the conclusion of the Haitian Revolution, he has been planning to start phase two—the export of the Haitian Revolution to the world. Grudgingly, I will admit that Afrika is a genius because I have known him since he was a child—a purchased slave by my late father. Our opponent is defined by boundless charisma, marvelous deceptive skills and a very strategic mind backed by a ferocious will. He is a clever fox that has influenced three revolutions: the American Revolution, the French Revolution, and the Haitian Revolution. The Black Fox must be hunted down before he instigates Armageddon—the World Revolution.

"I swore on my mother's grave when he killed most of my family that I would bring him back—dead or alive! Napoleon should have killed him instead of Toussaint. Afrika, when he met Boukman—not Toussaint—is singularly responsible for the loss of Haiti, which forced Napoleon to sell Louisiana to us. The nigger should not be underestimated! He must be stopped!"

The president cleared his throat and replied, "How reliable is your intelligence? You describe the ragtag Marshal...er, whatever his name is...as a one-man army or a weapon of mass destruction. Are we overestimating the fucking talents of a lowly nigger?"

Alexander Hamilton interjected, "General Elliott, aren't you taking the task too personal?"

General Elliott snarled, "Yes, I'm taking it personal, and America takes it personal, too, whenever a fucking nigger outgrows his breeches! The lowlife blacks are celebrating Afrika as the black messiah, the black Moses, the black Sir William Wallace, the black Dafydd ap Gruffudd, the black Spartacus, the black Arminius, and Hannibal. Shit, they have the audacity to compare the scum to Washington. I'm insulted, and America is insulted."

The president shouted, "OK, you made your point! What is your plan?"

The general answered, "Operation Black Fox entails the deployment of two snipers in Haiti."

Alexander Hamilton asked, "How reliable are these snipers?"

The general said, "They were personally trained by the legendary General John Stark—a former lieutenant to the late traitor Lieutenant Colonel Robert Rogers and his Rangers during the French and Indian War. This is the same great general who coined the famous motto of New Hampshire, the Granite State, 'Live free or die,' during our glorious struggle against the tyrannical regime of the Redcoats. A Haitian coon named Jacques Rene Chirac will be their guide. They will hide in the bushes by the grassy knoll where he rides to his office. Buyaka! Buyaka! Buyaka! Finally, they will conclude the hunt for the Black Fox."

The president, a glass of red wine in his hand, toasted, "Gentlemen, let's toast to a happy hunting!"

The general joked, "Actually, Afrika's head, as a trophy, would fit perfectly on the wall over your desk in the Oval Office, Mr. President."

Everyone responded with roaring laughter. Then the president sarcastically joked, "Yes, I always wanted to be known as the cannibal head-hunter president. Then my political opponents would call me the first black President. Ha! Ha! Ha!"

On my way to the Republican Guard headquarters, I was shot twice in my torso, and a bullet killed my favorite white steed. I returned fire and severely wounded my assailants. Bystanders took the wounded assassins and me to my headquarters. Immediately, I was treated for my wounds, and the snipers were tortured for information. Jacques Rene Chirac was arrested and beheaded in the town square. Monsieur Chirac's family was imprisoned, and his property was confiscated by the Republican Guard. The heads of the snipers were mailed to the White House with a note inscribed, "Mr. President, the Fox lives—signed by your darkest nightmare, Marshal Afrika Kenjo von Kunhardt."

In turn, the president pondered whether my note could be interpreted as a declaration of war. However, Dr. John Brown sent a memo to Alexander Hamilton and General Dick Elliott that Britain would not allow the United States of America to invade Haiti because Haiti was in her sphere of influence, and she would consider an American invasion as an expansion into her Caribbean backyard. In other words, she would consider an invasion of Jamaica's neighbor as an act of war. Secretly, Britain had designs on Haiti as a launching pad for the planned invasion of the United States of America. Presently, she was distracted by the war with France, and Dr. Brown, pressured by Sir Kevin Kirk Kinsley, temporarily suspended his abolitionist plans.

Dessalines and Tonnerre (newly promoted to marshal) were angry with me. They chastised me for my lack of a security detail. They feared I could have been killed. In their opinion, I was an indispensable asset to the young republic.

Unfortunately, my wounds became infected by contaminated horsehair when I was felled by the bullets. I sent for the best doctor in Jamaica to treat me. Colonel Henriques sent his personal physician, Dr. Ira Gutteres, to my bedside. He diagnosed my condition and stated that my spleen was damaged. In addition, I was slowly dying from a case of blood poisoning caused by foreign objects in my spleen. In resignation, he declared I had a few months to live.

At the sight of a white doctor hovering over me, Dessalines went into a fit of rage. He wondered, aloud, if I could trust a white doctor from Jamaica. I excused Dr. Gutteres from the room. Tonnerre, Petion, and Christophe joined us in my room. I told them the diagnoses. Their eyes became misty and saddened with the news of my report. Afterward, I commented on the need for us to import foreign expertise to modernize and Westernize Haiti. We should develop a five-year plan and invite experts to train indigenous talents in science, technology, education, and so forth. We needed to start rigorously educating our youth, both boys and girls, to sustain our revolution. For example, the Chinese taught the art of writing, science, and technology to the Mongols. Secondly, Western Europeans taught shipbuilding, modernization, and Western culture to Peter the Great's Russia. Thirdly, Prussians, under Baron von Steuben, taught drills and discipline to George Washington's troops. The Portuguese Jews taught sugar technology and "true" international commerce (built around slavery) to the British. We had to follow a Russian admiral's comment: "We have to learn our enemy's language." There was no need for us to reinvent the wheel if we could learn the technology from our neighbor because then, we would be able to overtake our neighbor more quickly in the game of world domination.

"Gentlemen, we need to temporarily import more Dr. Ira Guttereses to initiate our advance to world conquest."

Christophe and Petion agreed with my philosophy. Dessalines and Tonnerre were resistant—their hatred of whites was extremely great—but they understood the logic of my argument.

Dessalines appointed Tonnerre as the acting head of the Republican Guard. I willed my death mask to the Republican Guard, but I requested that my body be cremated. Next, I wanted Colonel Henriques to sprinkle my ashes throughout Jamaica—the birthplace of our first hero—Boukman. Moreover, I asked for a secretary to take my dictation as it pertained to my final will and testament and my memoirs.

Dessalines approved my requests. Before he left the room, he promised, "You will have a state funeral fit for an emperor. Afrika, you have an iron heart, and Mother Africa is proud of your achievements on her behalf. I vow that we'll continue to work hard to fulfill your dreams of a new and greater Africa."

I ordered Dr. Gutteres to fill my prescriptions and to import Jamaican ganja herbal tea to alleviate my agonizing pain. I requested German classical music and Jamaican roots and culture music to be played by various musicians outside my room. I hoped music would ease my anxieties and stress as the infection spread into my bloodstream.

Edouard Jean. *Toussaint Dirige Vers la Bataille*

In overthrowing me, you have cut only the trunk of the tree of liberty.
It will spring again from the roots for they are numerous and deep.

— TOUSSAINT L'OUVERTURE, 1802

Source: http://www.albany.edu/~js3980/haitian-revolution.html

10

AFRIKA'S UNCOMPROMISING VISION: HOLOCAUST TO HOMO SUPERIOR

W E ARE, SLOWLY, rising out of the ashes of the great holocaust of African slavery, due in part to our struggle for freedom. We must continue the struggle for our total freedom. The only way we can guarantee our freedom is a total war of preemptive strikes and defensive battles. We must continue the war until we achieve total domination—Homo Superior. Brilliantly, Napoleon has turned the French Revolution into a strategic platform to launch his ambition of world conquest. Secondly, the United States has turned the American Revolution into a strategic platform to launch its plan for world conquest (starting with its Manifest Destiny). Thirdly, the British Empire (under Oliver Cromwell) used the English Revolution (coupled with the Industrial Revolution) as a springboard toward world domination. Likewise, Mother Africa must use the Haitian Revolution as our road to our safety and security—world domination.

We should not halt our march to final victory, because our enemies will return us to slavery. For example, if we become content with the freedom of Haiti and dream of a peaceful coexistence with our neighbors, we cease exporting our revolution to the world. Our neighbors will isolate, invade, and occupy us. They will set up a puppet regime and steal our natural resources. They will turn our men into outlaws, our women into harlots, our children into beggars, and our nation into a rogue state. They will take our milk and honey. In turn, they will give us many barrels of liquor and devalue our money. They will turn us into indebted consumers of our own natural resources while they equate shameless thievery to astute productivity. Therefore, we must continue to fight.

Why do we fight? We fight to prevent our regression into mental slavery. Mental slavery is worse than physical slavery. For example, a healthy mind in a crippled body is free, while a crippled mind in a healthy body causes the body to be crippled because the mind controls the body. Therefore, an enslaved mind enslaves the physical body, while an enslaved body has the possibility of freedom via a free and inventive mind. Thus, we must free ourselves from mental slavery, and our body will follow suit. Again, we fight to final victory (over our enemies—the world) to secure our freedom, safety, and security.

Mother Africa is best served by subduing tribalism and placing states under a strong central government. In the United States of America, Alexander Hamilton (a native of the British West Indies) has been instrumental in his agenda to subdue states' rights under a strong central government. We have to be a united Africa. For example, Germany would be invincible if it could achieve unity by subjugating the diverse Germanic city-states under a strong German central government (e.g., Prussia).

Mother Africa is best served if she combines the positive traits of Sparta and Ancient Rome. She would be the perfect empire. Let's go further: Mother Africa should copy the best attributes of the following powers of the world of today: the British Empire; the French Empire; the Germanic nations, and the Jewish nation.

First, we need to copy the British Empire's skills of empire building and the art of naval warfare. Second, we need to duplicate the French Empire's skills of culture, philosophy, elegance, and revolutionary spirit. Third, we need to replicate the Germanic nations' Teutonic thoroughness and its military organizational skills (especially the Prussian army). Let's not forget, most of Napoleon's marshals and ministers are of German descent. For example, Marshal Ney is an ethnic German from the Alsace and Lorraine regions. Furthermore, Augustus Caesar's (and other Caesars') personal bodyguards were Germans, and Rome was unable to completely conquer Germania (while the great city of Rome was sacked by the inferior German barbarians). Fourth, we need to emulate the Jewish nation's skills for turning lemons into lemonade. They are able to survive pogroms and persecutions. They are able to be a part of a country and separate themselves from the country, concurrently. For good or ill, they collectively defend its ethnic community. After all, weren't Jesus and his apostles Jewish? Aren't Paul and Peter the giants of Christianity? Isn't the religion of Christianity (plus Roman law and German customs) the foundation of Western values? Jews contributed to the Golden Age of Islam (especially in Egypt and Spain) and the Italian Renaissance (via commerce, as a conduit for the exchange of ideas between cultures).

Despite the four powers' positive qualities, we have to view them as our enemies (competitors) because each of the Western powers is seeking the same goal out of its own self-interest. They hunger for power and thirst for money. They will preclude our survival and our pursuit of happiness—total domination. Mother Africa has to be wary of their deception, false religions, and self-serving ideas. They claim that what is good for them benefits humanity. In a Machiavellian way, Mother Africa must commit to what's to her people's benefit. Mother Africa must be benevolent to her allies, but she must be harsh on her foes and on herself. Africans, we must fight in the Name of God the Creator, in the name of pharaoh the man, and in the name of Africa the land because we cannot have peace without justice, nor justice without safety and security, nor safety and security without world conquest.

Never again will we live in slavery! Never again will we stand aside while they kill our prophets and our heroes. My mighty race—rise up and follow your prophets and heroes into the eternal battle for Mother Africa's survival, her birthright, and her imperial throne. Let your struggle be united with my struggle in the battle of Africa to bring about the birth of a nation—a nation to be called the United States of Africa (the African Empire). A nation that will be competing for world domination with the oppressive axis of Western civilization (the British Empire, the French Empire, and the Germanic Nations), with the Jewish nation serving as its point of origin.

In conclusion, the defeatist and the self-hating traitor (the domestic slave mentality) in us might think it is "mission: impossible" to defeat our competitors/

oppressors (the Jewish Nation, the Germanic Nations, the French Empire and the British Empire) and to conquer the world. To the defeatists, I'll quote one of my favorite heroes, the Carthaginian general Hannibal (BC 247–182): "We will either find a way, or make one."

United States of Africa/African Empire toward a greater Africa

Source: http://www2.richland2.org/rce/slavery.htm

ABOUT THE AUTHOR

K ARL A. MITCHELL was born and raised in Kingston, Jamaica. He is the product of a diverse heritage—the embodiment of Jamaica's motto: Out of many, one people. For example, his father's father's father was born and raised as a Jamaican Maroon, while his mother's mother's mother was born and raised as a Jew in Jamaica.

Academically, he has earned a bachelor's and two master's degrees. Currently, he is pursuing a doctorate.

Professionally, he is a consultant, lecturer, author, and entrepreneur.

Mr. Mitchell lives in New York.

Made in the USA
Middletown, DE
09 August 2023

36244458R00077